The Ninth Incarnation

Written and Illustrated by
Amanjot Kaur

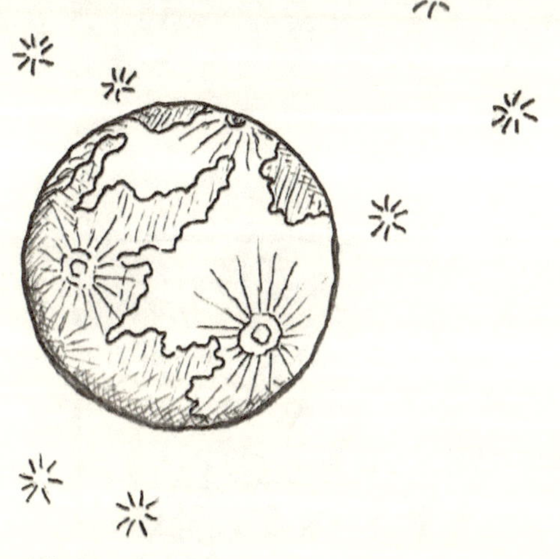

My beloved readers,

This tale hints at great truths,

But it is not the truth.

Remember it is a finger pointing toward the moon,

Not the moon itself.

CHAPTER 1

A STRANGER APPEARS

"TIME'S RUNNING OUT, SEAL!" AN URGENT VOICE shouted.

Seal snapped awake from deep sleep. The dream had returned with new intensity. The scraggly face, drooping whiskers, and voice were familiar from many dreams, but otherwise unknown to her. What did it mean? Why was time running out? For what? And why was that strange cat so desperate to get her attention?

Sitting up in her low wicker basket, she gazed around the empty kitchen. The only sound was the rhythmic dripping of the faucet. Stretching and yawning, Seal climbed out and padded her way to the big front porch, where she began grooming her long, white-and-gray fur.

Her nose twitched, sniffing the cool, moist air. Morning had come again to the old, three-story house with wide bands of dark green and purple shingles wrapped around it. The base of the structure was much wider than the top, making it look like it was being stretched upward, about to be sucked into the sky. On one corner, a turret pointed like an arrow toward some unknown destination. The massive chestnut tree to the east was bursting with new leaves. Rusty-vested robins danced in and out of the old iron fence that encircled the large grassy yard.

Seal had come to the cat orphanage as a small kitten. Vague memories from the time before her eyes had opened haunted her occasionally. A large, warm shape grasping her firmly by the neck flap. The sensation of swinging freely while being carried. Nestling among other tiny, warm, wriggling shapes that cried out in soft, high-pitched meows. The earthy scent of her mother… That was all she remembered of her life before.

This was the last year she would be able to live there. Cats were not allowed to stay past the age of four. She was done with her schooling and was expected to help out as a member of staff until autumn, when she would be forced to leave for good. Her days were monotonous with cooking meals for several dozen kitten residents and staff along with doing other household chores.

The looming future left her feeling sad and frightened. *I have no idea where I'll go or what I'll do*, she thought as she sat looking across the yard. Life would soon become difficult in many ways. She had no money, family, or friends. Somehow, she would have to find a place to live and learn how to take care of herself. Her body heaved out a heavy sigh, weighed down by uncertainty and dread of the unknown future.

During kittenhood, life had seemed magical and full of possibilities. She remembered experiencing many wonderful moments back then. Once, while watching a blazing orange and purple sunset from high in a tree, she had become very still. Her eyes had dilated like saucers, and there was a tingling in her spine and brain. She'd felt a powerful sensation that everything was perfect. Somehow, even the facts that she was alone with no family, scrawny, and had received detention earlier that day for misbehaving were part of the perfection. She couldn't understand or explain this to anyone. She'd just known deep inside that it was true. In that moment, everything had felt part of one inseparable, faultless whole.

Another day during school, she had felt the magic in a different way. She had gone out for afternoon recess and wandered off alone like usual. While all the other kittens were playing and making lots of noise, Seal sat still, staring off into the horizon. She relaxed her weight down into her haunches, and her eyes remained open. The next thing she knew, everyone had disappeared. Recess had ended, and she had no idea how long ago. The yard was completely empty and still. How had she not noticed the bell ringing or the kittens all scurrying back inside? Time had seemed to stop or disappear when all that noisiness was going on. The experience was a profound mystery. At the time, she hadn't stopped to puzzle over it. She just hurried inside, hoping the teacher wouldn't yell at her for being late.

Other times, when she'd been exploring the small

plantation of trees north of the orphanage, which she called "the forest," she had felt waves of something indescribable. It seemed like all the love in the world was bursting forth from her head and chest. Seal noticed the way the leaves of the trees shimmered in the breeze and the sunlight dappled through them.

The smell of sweet grass and pungent olive trees was carried on the wind and wrapped itself around her. Nothing else mattered other than what she was experiencing. She knew that these simple things everyone else was too busy to notice were actually the most important things of all. She felt like she could have sprouted wings and flown into the sky, savoring the experience of life flowing.

While at the pond one day, Seal had been swept over by another strange yet wonderful experience. She'd been sitting in the shade, gazing at the deep greenish water, rocks, and trees swaying overhead. A loon's cry crossed the water from the far side. Two kingfishers were perched high in the overhanging trees. They shot down below the water's surface at alternating intervals, expertly catching minnows. She'd been struck by the knowledge that within all these things, the same source of existence was pulsing. Somehow the wind, the emerald water, the swaying branches, the sounds of the loon, the kingfishers' movements, and even an old, crumpled chewing-gum wrapper tumbling along in the breeze before her, sparkled with a oneness that seemed to say, "I, Life, am living in *all* these things."

There's also something special about sunlight, she'd decided as she walked slowly back home. *Some hidden intelligence and power in it. When it moves and flashes, I feel something alive.* She had especially loved seeing it dance in golden waves on the ceiling, when it reflected off a watery surface. Mesmerized, she would sit watching it, feeling that some silent communication was happening in a language she didn't know. She sensed it was trying to remind her that she was part of something greater than she could imagine.

Seal remembered how Supervisor Mota had marched the kittens to the local church every Sunday. Sitting on the long, hard bench every week, she had listened to the preacher speak but never feeling anything in her heart—even though she'd wanted to. However, when the sunlight felt alive or she had those special moments in nature, something powerful had spread throughout her whole being. *I think this is what the preacher is trying to talk about. But there really are no words for it.* She'd then drifted into a funny daydream about the preacher stopping midsermon to pull a sun hat out from under the pulpit, and directing the congregation to move outside and explore the meadow that opened out behind the little wooden church.

As time went by, Seal had experienced the magic less and less, until it almost stopped completely. Now, rarely, the sunlight still spoke to her of that belonging and feeling that somehow everything was perfect. Mostly, her mind and heart felt very heavy, and she dreaded the moment her eyes would open each morning.

Seal's memories of the past faded as she looked out over the lawn. Then she thought again about the old cat in her dream. Who was he, and what could it possibly mean? Again, the voice echoed in her head, *"Time is running out, Seal!"*

"Seal... Seal!" This time it was a real voice, roaring from inside the house.

Another sigh escaped her as she turned to go back inside. Supervisor Mota was charging down the wide carved staircase, which groaned and creaked under his weight.

"Breakfast should have been ready by now!" he reprimanded her with his deep voice. "Get in the kitchen and take this parcel with you." A grin spread across his face from ear to ear. "Bija and Spooks showed superior skill in their mousing exam yesterday. Give them these as a reward." He held out a small, pink paperboard box and plunked it into Seal's outstretched paws. She immediately recognized it as being from the pastry shop.

Back in the kitchen, she dropped the box on the old wooden table, then placed a huge pot on the range

to prepare some porridge. Her stormy blue eyes shone back from the pot's surface, burning with anger and jealousy. The white-and-gray flame mark on her forehead seemed to quiver like live fire.

Once the oats were boiling, she returned to the table and slowly opened the box. Inside, two fish-shaped marzipan cakes had been carefully placed on lacy lining paper. The cream-and-raspberry-filled cakes were Seal's favorite. She never got them anymore. Opening the small cupboard above the mantel, she bitterly shoved the box inside, then returned to the porridge.

Moments later, two rowdy kittens burst through the swinging door in a tumble of furry excitement. "Seal, Supervisor Mota said you have a surprise for us!" Their green-and-yellow eyes sparkled with excitement as they sat eagerly awaiting their reward.

Seal opened the cupboard and peered into the darkness. Pushing aside the pink box, she took out an old container of stale fish crackers, then poured them into the open paws of the thrilled youngsters.

"Wow, this is the best!" They smiled as they munched on big mouthfuls, then ran back out the door.

Grabbing the pastry box, she opened it greedily. Within moments, the cakes were devoured. Pain shot through her stomach as she stared at the empty container. *They didn't even taste that good.* Her head hung with shame and guilt. *Everything beautiful seems gone from life!* Crumpling the box with fury, she pushed it deep into the trash bin.

When the oats were ready, she served the meowing

kittens in the dining room. After a few hours of work cleaning the orphanage, she returned to the kitchen, feeling dejected. There was still a huge mess from breakfast. Forty-five minutes later, the dirty mountain of dishes was cleaned up. Seal finally sat down and began licking oatmeal spatter from her fur.

A cool breeze, perfumed with wild violets, wafted through the cracked window. Seal looked across the ruddy brick floor to where her sleeping basket was warming in the afternoon glow. Sighing, she crept over and curled up inside. *Maybe a nap will bring relief,* she thought hopefully. But as she lay, she couldn't ignore an aching, sick emptiness in her heart.

The edges of sleep had barely reached her when she was jolted awake. She was being watched. Her eyes grew wide as she scanned the room…nothing. *Drip, drip,* the faucet continued. The thin curtain waved, ghostlike in the delicate breeze. The kitchen was desolate and sleepy. *I must be imagining it,* she thought as she closed her eyes tightly and nestled her face under her paw. Then, the silence was suddenly pierced by a tiny, powerful, and unfamiliar voice.

"I have been sent by the Great Teacher to get you. Too much time has already been wasted. Pack your things, Seal. We must leave immediately!"

Seal's eyes snapped open in shock. Fixing her gaze on the shelf above the fireplace, she saw a small brown mouse, sporting a conspicuously long, white beard. *If it weren't for all that facial hair, he might be a good snack,* she thought.

"Who are you? How do you know my name?" Leaping out of her basket, she began questioning the peculiar messenger. "Where do you want me to go? And who's the Great Teacher?" Then, pausing to eye the plump mouse again, she added, "Is your beard fake?"

The little rodent zipped down the mantel and, in seconds, was readying his sharp teeth millimeters away from her snowy-white back foot.

"Hey!" Seal shouted. "What's this about?" She steadily eyed the mysterious creature. The mouse's black eyes glistened like polished glass beads and were filled with fiery intensity. His soft, quivering beard pointed downward in a wavy triangle. It looked like it could have been made of sheep's wool or cotton.

"I'm Mukti, master of maps. Too much time is being wasted. Are you coming or not? It doesn't make any difference to me."

Seal was trying to get past her shock and make sense of the situation. Her eyes stared off blankly into the distance while she considered her options. *I don't know this mouse. Maybe he's just a lunatic. But what is there to stay for? More days of emptiness and drudgery, while the clock counts down to my being put out on the street? Maybe this "Great Teacher," whoever he is, will be able to help me find a job or something.*

"Okay…" she replied with hesitation. "Let's go."

"Pack lightly," Mukti ordered.

Opening a tall wooden cupboard, Seal took her canvas travel bag and jacket from a peg, then carefully packed a few meager belongings. She filled an embroidered pouch with dried fish and fruit snacks, a packet

of rice, and the wooden cooking paddle she had carved the previous summer.

"That's it—we're off!" Mukti cheered as Seal closed her pack.

She paused a moment, surveying the warm kitchen before closing the door for the last time. Her heart felt curious but far from cheerful.

"Where to?" she asked Mukti.

"To the coast. The Cat Ship awaits."

CHAPTER 2

THE CAT SHIP

BEFORE THE AFTERNOON HAD PASSED, THE TWO UN-likely companions left the landscape of lawns, trees, and village behind and arrived at the coast. Sunlight flashed on waves of choppy water.

Seal's eyes narrowed from the brightness. The scent of the sea was strong and fresh. Her long whiskers bristled with exhilaration at the smells wafting to her little gray nose. Salt, fish, seaweed, and wet sand warmed by the sun. *This is delightful!* she mused.

"There she is, the Cat Ship." Mukti pointed a tiny paw forward.

Docked at the shore was an old, brown wooden boat. It was as big as a whale and had the whimsical shape of a pirate ship. Seal eyed it with suspicion. *It looks ready for the graveyard, not a long voyage.*

Two rows of circular windows lined the length of the vessel, each sporting colorful printed curtains. *Well, maybe I'll get a cabin with purple or peacock-colored drapes,* she thought hopefully.

They joined the line of passengers who were slowly moving inside. Animals of all different species were gathered for the journey.

As they reached the top of the boarding plank, Seal poked the side of the ship with her paw and felt her stomach sink. The wood squished like a soaked sponge. "Where are we going, Mukti? How long do we have to be onboard this thing?"

"First stop is the coast of China, but that's not our final destination. The Cat Ship should get there in about twenty days. Provided we have smooth sailing."

Mukti handed over two paper slips to the shipmaster, who stamped them in red before allowing them to board.

"I never thought I would see the Orient," Seal remarked.

Mukti smiled as he scampered into the ship.

Looking behind her one last time, Seal gazed at the landscape. *I'm leaving the only home I've ever known. Maybe I'll never see it again.* Her stomach felt weak, her mouth was quivering, and her eyes glistened with tears. Blinking hard, she turned, then entered the ship's dark interior.

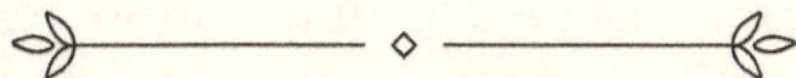

Following Mukti down a long wooden passage, she paused now and then to peek inside the open doorways of the cabins. Surprisingly, they were bright and cheerful. Some had tables with flowered cloths. Some had puffy beds with colorful covers printed with dragonflies or rabbits. It was all very lovely. *Maybe this journey won't be so bad after all,* she considered optimistically.

On and on they went, downstairs and along another hallway. One corner of her mouth fell as she noticed that the cabins here were not quite so nice as the ones above. *Well, maybe I'll still get a room with the color of curtains I like best,* she thought in an effort to stay positive.

The lighting had become dim as they continued down one last flight of creaking stairs. Seal's nose crinkled from a strong musty smell. The next room was different. They were in the ship's large belly. *No windows at all!* she realized in alarm while scanning the dark, lamplit chamber. Rows of dirty hammocks hung from the walls.

"Here we are!" Mukti announced happily.

Grubby-looking passengers were slowly entering, finding their assigned spots, and stowing their luggage before settling in. Some were sleeping or reading. A mother rabbit was busy rocking her small baby. Some other babies were crying in another corner of the ship's cavernous shadows. All in all, it was a grim scene.

Mukti directed Seal to a hammock, then climbed into the one above it. While placing her travel bag on the ground, she began reconsidering her decision to go on this journey.

Each hammock had a thin cotton blanket, more like a sheet. The room was dark, and the blankets were so dirty that Seal had to squint to see that hers was covered with a dragonfly pattern. Pawing at the cloth sadly, she noticed a small, clean section along the edge. *Once, long ago, it was a beautiful turquoise color.* She sighed. As she jumped into the hammock, she called up to Mukti, "These are going to be long days."

However, time passed quickly and not as she expected. Not long after the Cat Ship set sail, the rocking motion of the boat began to make her violently ill. Up and down, round and round. She felt like she couldn't get her bearings. The hammock didn't help, as it was constantly swinging. Seal spent the first night throwing up. After that, the journey became a strange series of blurry memories.

Sometimes she would wake to find Mukti at her side, pouring water into her parched mouth. Other times he would be trying to push a cracker or porridge into her muzzle. Once, she awoke to the sight of a baby rabbit with large brown eyes silently studying her over the edge of her hammock. Seal watched it through hot, watery eyes, not knowing if it was real or a dream. The greasy lamplight kept everything obscure, and the only constant was that everything seemed to keep spinning, spinning.

Twenty-nine days after boarding the ship, it pulled into the dock on the coast of China. Seal and Mukti deboarded with the last of the passengers, then stood on shore, squinting at the midday sun. She clutched a blanket around her shoulders. Her body had become thin, and her fur drooped. Her tail hung limply, and it took a lot of effort to walk.

"Where to now?" she asked, her voice just above a whisper.

"Ghandruk, in the Himalayas," Mukti energetically replied.

"Grand Truck? Where?" Seal was puzzled.

The shipmaster then announced that passengers traveling on to the Himalayas should wait on the opposite dock, where their ship would arrive in fifteen minutes. Seal and Mukti made their way over and sat down in the long, soft, windblown grass to wait. Their noses twitched, inhaling the sweet, fresh smell. The cool air, solid ground, and warm sunlight felt like heaven.

Seal gazed out over the ocean. "I want this traveling to be finished—before it finishes me!"

Mukti chuckled, then they both became silent.

Fifteen minutes, the shipmaster said. I should be able to see the next ship coming, but there's nothing anywhere in sight, she pondered, then glanced down at Mukti, who seemed to be in a sort of trance. The mouse's eyes were open a sliver, paws resting on his legs. His breath was almost still, but his beard quivered in the breeze.

Pulling the blanket tighter around her, Seal continued watching the horizon and worrying about the future. Time slowly passed, and eventually, she slouched forward into a doze.

Several minutes later, she woke up and straightened herself to survey the ocean's surface again, this time with more concern. *It's got to have been more than fifteen minutes!* Yet the sea was still empty but for rolling waves.

After some time, a clanging bell sounded, startling them both. The Cat Ship had begun moving away from the dock.

"No! The other ship hasn't arrived," Seal cried frantically. "If this one leaves, we will be stuck here!"

Mukti didn't seem concerned, which frustrated her even more. They watched as the departing Cat Ship moved away from shore, then slowly turned and began approaching them again, gliding into the dock where the next ship was to arrive.

"What?" she called out angrily. "I am *not* getting back on that thing!"

"We aren't getting back on that," Mukti replied. "Wait."

Just then, a series of popping sounds filled the air, and something began to move. Seal saw the body of the Cat Ship starting to bulge. "Is it disintegrating?" No, but the bulging continued. "It's going to explode! Run, Mukti, run!" Seal got up, but Mukti wouldn't budge.

"Look, Seal." The ship's entire frame was distended, now bulging to the point of looking like a balloon. A soft, transparent top was expanding over the deck.

Seal squinted, observing the changes. The clear covering above the ship reflected rainbow tones where it curved. *It looks like the soap bubbles I used to blow.* The unusual craft now slowly began to rise from the water.

"The Cat Ship is also an air vessel," Mukti explained, his two front teeth a flash of white as he smiled.

"Wow," she whispered.

The bell clanged again, and the shipmaster reappeared. "All passengers, please board."

Mukti and Seal's tickets were stamped, this time with blue, and they climbed on board.

"How long is this part of the journey?" she asked with concern.

"We should reach the village by evening," Mukti serenely replied.

There were seats around the edge of the deck. Mukti showed Seal where to sit. She could look out at everything from this vantage point. The dome overhead offered views of sunlight and beautiful, puffy clouds. Seal stowed her travel bag under her seat and settled in. Mukti left and returned with some water for her.

"Thank you," Seal said, realizing that Mukti had shown her more care in their short time together than she had experienced in years.

The final bell clanged as the last passengers boarded. Then the ship began to lift farther and farther from the ground. Seal could see the objects below rapidly turn doll sized, then ant sized, then completely disappear from view.

They traveled westward. Rivers, desert plains, and forests followed each other in quick succession. The warm sun continued to move across the sky.

Seal enjoyed the scenery as long as she could, but eventually her still-weary body gave in, and she succumbed to a deep sleep.

The next thing she knew, Mukti was poking her belly. Her eyes opened to a sunset-filled sky of orange-and-yellow clouds. The Cat Ship had landed in a grassy clearing.

"Final destination," Mukti squeaked.

Stretching and yawning, Seal unfurled from her seat, then they departed the Cat Ship one last time. Grateful to be on solid ground again, she paused to take in the scene. They were in a meadow on top of a mountain. Spinning around in a slow circle, she marveled at the grand snow-covered peaks that dotted the horizon in all directions. Closer to the ground, mist hung in pockets. Seal shivered from the cold air. It was beautiful, but the unfamiliar surroundings sent a wave of fear through her.

"I have some urgent business to attend to," Mukti

suddenly announced. "You will have to walk to the monastery yourself." Pulling a blank parchment and thick pencil from his bag, he speedily began drafting a map. "Cross the village, then up the slope and terrace to here." He traced the route with his paw. "It is a bit far, but the path is easy to follow. I'll be heading in the opposite direction."

They bid each other farewell, and she sadly watched Mukti depart across the meadow. Seal stood staring, unsure of what to do and feeling very alone in this strange land. Her stomach grumbled loudly. *I need food.* There was still a beautiful sunset glow lighting her way as she headed off on the pathway indicated by the map.

A village began to sprout up around her. Small lanes were lined with homes and shops selling various things. Seal's heart began to lighten, and she felt enchanted by the square, bright-colored prayer flags, which were strung up everywhere.

Continuing on, she soon found herself in a crowd of villagers. Struggling to make her way forward, Seal pressed tightly between all the moving bodies, but the motion of the marketgoers was like a churning ocean. She was spun around and jostled this way and that until she'd completely lost her sense of direction. Her face pinched as she mustered the strength to get out of the living whirlpool. But the crowd had shifted again and was parting in a different direction. Suddenly, Seal was forcefully ejected into the open. Looking up in disbelief, she froze.

Standing in a clearing some yards off was the old, wise-looking cat she had seen in her dreams. The same one who had called out to her so urgently, saying that "time is running out." His scraggly face, drooping whiskers, and sharp, intelligent eyes that had come to her scores of times during sleep were now staring at her in reality. He beckoned to her.

How can he be real? Seal thought, overcome with wonder as she began inching forward.

Smiling softly, the old cat reached out and gently placed a gray paw on her head. "I've waited long for you, little one. Come."

CHAPTER 3

THE GREAT TEACHER

THE ANCIENT-LOOKING CAT TURNED, AND THEY CONTINued on in silence for some time. As they passed through the village, the sky darkened into deep purples and blues. Eventually, they crossed into wild, open country. The ribbon of earth Seal was walking on felt like a highway in the sky.

"Are you the Great Teacher?" she asked hesitantly.

Her companion burst forth in a powerful, hearty laugh that took her by surprise. "Mukti!" He sighed, shaking his head, then continued, "Please, call me Tansen."

"Tansen," Seal echoed. The name felt like a delicate bell ringing in her memory. Somehow it seemed near and dear to her.

His beautiful burgundy- and mustard-colored robes made swishing sounds as he effortlessly sped onward. Seal was pressing herself to keep up with his quick pace. *I feel ready to collapse,* she thought as hunger pains cramped painfully in her belly.

The landscape was sweepingly vast. In many places, the trail was almost overgrown with low brush. *I'm glad I'm not alone.* She sighed as they made their way to the remote destination. *Without a guide, I might have wandered off and gotten lost.*

They had traveled for almost two hours through inky darkness when something caught her attention. In the far distance, the glow of small, yellow lights appeared. They were nearing the monastery.

Following a narrow pathway of stones, they arrived at a low stone building. Seal could smell patches of pungent marigolds nearby.

Just outside the door, under a large tree, her knees buckled as her stomach convulsed tightly. Grinding her teeth together, Seal held her breath while a powerful wave of pain overwhelmed her. Sinking down like a wet noodle, she glanced up. Tansen was bending over her with deep concern in his eyes. Her vision closed in like collapsing tunnels, then everything went dark.

The next thing she knew, she was sensing brightness through her closed eyelids. Opening them slowly, she squinted. *It's morning!*

She was lying on a bed. Sitting up slowly, Seal looked around the small room. A low table stood beneath the bare window, and her travel bag and jacket had been hung on a peg by the door. She glanced down at her belly as it rippled and rumbled from hunger. *Other than my starving stomach, I feel pretty good.* She smiled to herself. Slinking out of bed, she opened the heavy wooden door just enough to peek out. There was silence and stillness, but the delicious smells of cooking wafted pleasantly toward her.

Cautiously, Seal crept from the room and down the hallway. Padding silently through an open foyer, she paused in a large doorway to look inside. Saffron-robed monks were busy working around a table. *Food!* she thought, hurrying forward. She gently pushed her way between their bodies to reach the table.

There was no food. Curious and beautiful, the monks were each holding long metal cones in one hand and pencil-shaped metal rods in the other. They were rubbing the rods against bumpy ridges on the cones. From the small ends of the cones, colorful sand was being skillfully laid on the table in beautiful, intricate patterns. They were making some kind of picture. The monks were concentrating intensely and didn't notice their visitor.

Backing away slowly, Seal continued her quest for food. Following the compass of her twitching nose, she wound her way through the halls. Finally, she came to another large chamber with long tables, where breakfast had been laid out. A friendly looking monk waved hello.

Seal grinned at him as she sat down on a bench. She didn't even have time to look around before a metal plate of food was brought to her. There were large chunks of potato covered in red spices and a round mountain of rice to the side. Chewing each mouthful as long as she could, she savored the unusual flavors. *This is the best thing I've eaten in over a month!* she thought as she scooped another large spoonful into her mouth.

Tansen arrived as she was finishing the last bites. The white parts of her face were now orange from the spices.

"Come with me, Seal." He chuckled.

Reluctantly, she left her plate and followed the old cat to his study. Firm cushions of colorful silk covered the floor. Tansen pointed Seal toward one and then sat across from her.

"What's that wonderful picture they are making on the table?" Seal asked.

"It's a mandala. A sort of picture of the entire Universe," Tansen answered.

Seal puzzled over that silently for a few moments, then asked, "Why did Mukti bring me here?"

"You have a difficult task to complete. But first you must learn to be in stillness."

Seal stared back, confused. What could the task

possibly be? And learning stillness? After thinking a moment, she replied, "But I was in stillness every day at the orphanage, in the sunspot on the kitchen floor."

"You must learn to experience your *mind* from stillness," Tansen said.

Puzzled, she stared down at the floor.

"Seal," he resumed, "many things are possible when our awareness becomes fully opened."

She looked at him questioningly.

"Have you ever noticed how your mind moves around like a monkey?"

Seal thought about what her mind had been doing the past several minutes. First, she had been thinking about what was going to happen while sitting with Tansen. The idea of completing a difficult task had reminded her of being stuck on the roof of the cat orphanage when she was small. After that, her mind had flitted to the present, as the movement of a moth caught her eye. That triggered a memory of chasing butterflies when she was a kitten. She had pondered over what on earth Tansen meant by *awareness* and *stillness*, then begun thinking about leaving the orphanage, which spiraled into thoughts about the journey that had brought her here. *Wow, my mind really did go everywhere, just like a monkey,* she realized in amazement. Not only that—she felt her body had been flooded with a range of emotions as the thoughts had passed through her mind. Her arms, legs, and tail had become tense, and her stomach was clenched.

"Many secrets of the mind, body, and Universe are to be found by bringing attention to your awareness."

Tansen continued, "Gaze up at your brow flame and breathe. Concentrate on your breath. Make it deep and long. Sit up straight and listen deeply. Seal," he directed in a gentle tone, "don't fight the flow of thoughts that come. Just observe… Don't grab on to them. Don't board them like a train. Just let them go…"

Seal took slow, deep breaths, focusing her attention on the gray-and-white flame of fur above her nose. One after another, thoughts kept coming and going. Thoughts about anything and everything. Pretend conversations from an imagined future. Memories of past events, sometimes with new endings. Thoughts about what was happening right now. *Wow, I must have thousands of thoughts every single day!* she marveled. It was like a huge river that just kept flowing.

Seal did her best just to observe it all. Her body became tense if she grabbed on to any thought—even a small one. Sometimes a lot of time went by before she realized she was on the thought train again. Then she would tremble, exhale, and let her mind babble on without listening to it. Deep relaxation spread through-out her body.

"Seal, are you the thoughts? Are you the feelings?" Tansen asked.

She knit her brow, considering the old cat's question. "I never thought about it before."

Silently, she examined her experiences. "I've always felt guilty if angry or bad thoughts came into my mind. I have believed that the thoughts are me…or that I am the thoughts."

But here she was, some part of her watching steadily as all the thoughts and feelings flooded by endlessly. They came and went, came and went. She couldn't say where they had come from, and she didn't know where they went when they left. She realized with amazement that part of her was separate from them, steadily observing. Whatever she was, it never came or went. *Wow!* she thought, then realized that was another thought, coming and now going.

What about the feelings she experienced? Was she the feelings? She began to look at her own experiences again. "I remember times of happiness and joy coming. Also, days with anger, fear, and loneliness."

Tansen's eyes were sparkling like diamonds as he nodded encouragingly for her to continue.

Seal became quiet as she realized that both the pleasant and unpleasant feelings had all passed away into some unknown, unseeable region. *I wonder where they go when I am not feeling them?* she asked herself. But more interesting was that she never came or went with those feelings. Whatever she was, it was something more stable—permanent.

Tansen closed his eyes, and they continued the practice of sitting in stillness, letting the thoughts go by.

Thirty minutes had sped by on the clock before he spoke again, "Have you noticed anything strange about your memories, Seal? Come now…focus. Spine straight, tail relaxed. Breathe…so deep, so slow, it's silent."

She followed Tansen's directions and began to see images in her mind. "I'm on a hillside, planting cam-

phor trees in strange, high wooden sandals. My friend is with me…"

"Yes, good… What else?"

"Now we are in a different land, a desert under a starry sky. We're wearing long robes and tall caps on our heads. We're twirling, twirling and spinning in ecstasy!"

"Continue!" Tansen's eyes became large, and he leaned forward, listening to Seal with growing excitement.

"Now we're in a different place with high mountains. My friend and I are making a sand picture—a mandala, like those monks."

"Hmmm, very good—and?"

"We are laughing and crossing a bridge in an ancient forest. Special sticks with strange writing on them are poking out of the water. We're entering a shrine with ten thousand lanterns…"

"More, keep going. Spine straight, keep your focus."

"Now we are far from the deserts, mountains, and forests. We're near a large, sacred pool of water. There's a golden temple in the center. I see a man with a long, black beard. His face radiates warmth like the sun… He's giving my friend fragrant leaves called tulsi…" Seal's voice trailed off as the memories faded.

Tansen chuckled knowingly. "Very good. Progress." His face crinkled as he smiled. "Your friend, whom you forgot, do you remember him now?"

"Ardaas," Seal said. "How could I have forgotten him? But this doesn't make sense. I have been at the orphanage since kittenhood. I've never been to any of those strange places. I've never had a close friend. I was alone back home… Why didn't I remember these things before? What's going on?"

Seal was frightened. The images had been as detailed and clear as daylight. Yet they contained objects, places, and a friend she had never known before. She felt instinctively that there was truth in them. The memories felt familiar and beloved, but how could they be real?

Tansen looked at her steadily then replied in a serious tone, "Have you ever heard the saying that cats have nine lives?"

Seal recalled the time when she had gotten stuck fifty feet off the ground in a massive elm tree near the orphanage. One of the rescue workers had said something about nine lives when she was back on the ground. Tilting her head, she asked, "Doesn't it just mean cats are lucky and able to do adventurous things?"

"No, Seal, it means quite a bit more than that," Tansen replied as he fixed her in his intense stare. "You have lived eight previous lives as a cat. Those were all memories from your past lives. You are now in your ninth life. This time, when you leave your cat body at the time of death, you will no longer return to it. You will transform, as is the will of the Divine. That change may make it impossible for you to find and save Ardaas." Tansen's paws clenched his knees tightly as he leaned in toward Seal. "You must try to find him and save him this one last time. After all, you and Ardaas have been friends since the time before time and for many lifetimes. Just as I have been your teacher many times."

More questions were popping up. "Why does Ardaas need saving? How can I find him?" Nervously twisting her paws together, she fell silent, then shifted her weight on the cushion before adding, "I do feel a great sadness. I feel he is lost. Like part of me is missing. But how can that be? I have never known Ardaas in this life—I would remember that!"

"Quite correct, in this lifetime you were separated early. The destructive gorilla Kadir has taken Ardaas captive. He has parted you for many lifetimes. He has killed Ardaas many times."

"Killed!" Seal shuddered.

"Yes, and he plans to do so again. His heart and mind have been poisoned by his envy and jealousy of the friendship and love between you and Ardaas. Kadir's mind has chewed over hateful thoughts for so long that he is blind to everything but his desire to destroy the bond between the two of you." Tansen's voice had risen in intensity and speed, his eyes becoming large and expressive. "You're running out of time, Seal. You must follow the trail to Ardaas before it's too late. Through your soul connection and with the discipline of your mind and body, you may have the ability to find him. Do you remember him enough to do that?"

So this was the difficult task. Seal knit her brow and squinted as she concentrated on the images she had seen in her mind—her past lives with Ardaas. "I think so." Her tone was hopeful. "He's orange-and-cream colored…and fluffy like me!"

"No, I think not." Tansen's face sank into a look of worried concern. "You are remembering his last cat life. His ninth life has passed, and he transformed as the Divine willed. You must find him by remembering his soul, not his shell."

Seal looked up with great worry, trembling. "I don't know if I can."

"You must. You have mastered many things in your lives, Seal. You must remember and regain your skills. Find the places Ardaas was before. He may be there now." Tansen paused, then continued in hushed tones, "If you fail this time, all is lost."

"Will you come with me and help me?" Seal widened her eyes as she pleaded.

"I cannot. It is not my dharma. You must complete this yourself. There will be others to help along the way—you're not alone."

"What is dharma?" Seal asked. She didn't seem to understand anything anymore.

"It's a path through this life, Seal. Your soul's path given by the Divine."

"What or who is the Divine?" she asked, even more puzzled.

"The Divine is not a thing or a being," Tansen replied. "The Divine is everything and nothing. All intelligence, coordination, forms, and phenomenon arise and fall away in the Divine. All experience and nonexperience…"

Experience and nonexperience? Seal stared at her teacher, not understanding a word he had said.

"Don't worry, Seal. You don't need to understand this with your mind." Smiling, her ancient teacher stood up and continued in happier tones, "After some time, Mukti will arrive to guide you to your next destination. Remember to follow his instructions. They come from me."

"Yes, sir." Seal sighed as she slouched over, looking at the ground. All she could do was trust and surrender. She felt the challenges of this mysterious new reality stacking up against her.

"Today, you will work and help in the kitchen. Tomorrow we will meet again to continue your studies."

She sighed with relief. These were two things she still understood.

Seal made her way to the kitchen, where she was given a small apron. She was surprised by how wonderful it could feel to work hard. Back at the orphanage, chores had always felt like a punishment. But now, there was a great joy in sweating alongside the monks of the monastery. Vegetables were chopped, lunch prepared, pots and pans cleaned, and the floors swept and scrubbed. Her fellow workers were quiet and radiated a peaceful joy. It felt like nourishment just to be near them.

One of them had a large smile and twinkling eyes. He exuded a gentle happiness that seemed to have no particular cause. *That seems like something important to grow—the ability to feel joy for no specific reason,* she decided.

Later, Seal wandered back to see the progress of

the sand mandala. It had been completed. She stood staring at each delicate detail, a mathematical and artistic perfection of beauty. Suddenly, Tansen stepped toward it. He calmly stretched out a paw and began swiping through the mandala, effectively destroying it with each pass.

"No! What are you doing?" Seal called out. The other monks were standing by, watching the destruction without any alarm.

Her teacher's voice was calm. "All things have their time, little one. The Universe is not permanent."

Bewildered, Seal wandered sadly from the hall out into the blue dusk. *The mandala was so beautiful! Why did Tansen ruin it?* She gazed out over the mighty Himalayas, which were now just jagged outlines of black against the darkening night sky. The cold wind tousled her fur. She sat near the marigold patch until darkness had closed in completely. The vastness of the starry sky opened before her. Gazing up, she felt like a drop in the ocean.

CHAPTER 4

MASTER AND STUDENT

Before she knew it, Seal had been at the monastery for a few months. Time seemed to pass faster here.

One day after lunch, she sat, contemplating, on a hillside that overlooked the expansive wilderness. *Maybe this place is in a magical vortex where time is warped.*

She remembered a recent session she'd had with Tansen. She had looked at the clock when they'd sat down—7:07 p.m. Her eyes had been open, and she'd gazed at her teacher as he meditated, his eyes fixed downward. A few minutes passed. Then he inquired in a soft, relaxed voice, "Seal, what time is it?"

She had looked up in confusion and disbelief. The clock read 7:41 p.m. But it had just been a few minutes! She was sure of it. Tansen returned to his inner state of focus while she stared at him, wondering what had just happened. *Yes,* she mused, *this place is very strange at times.*

Seal surveyed the mountains that arose on all sides.

Inhaling in short sniffs, she savored the fresh, earthy scents. Her paw softly brushed the tiny pink-and-white flowers dotting the surface of the grass as she continued thinking about her life at the monastery.

She had learned that Tansen and the monks practiced something called Buddhism. However, her teacher wasn't afraid to mix in things he'd learned from other traditions now and then, *if* he felt they were beneficial. Seal liked that. But she'd been told that sometimes other temple officials gave him trouble because of his open-mindedness.

Every day, Seal and Tansen practiced being in a state of quiet stillness and awareness while their thoughts and emotions flowed on. Some days the river of thoughts was roaring and loud. Some days it was so placid she forgot it was there, or it disappeared completely. At other times, her thoughts became like the sounds of someone talking in a distant room—too soft to make out distinctly. The old cat had also begun teaching her some difficult breathing exercises.

"Inhale for a count of twenty seconds, Seal."

She tried, but she breathed in too quickly, and her lungs were completely filled by ten seconds. She felt like she was going to burst as she spent the next ten seconds trying to suck more air in.

"Now suspend the breath for twenty seconds. Don't let any of it out."

This part felt surprisingly easy to her. She became very still.

"Now exhale, but make sure it takes another twenty seconds before the breath is out," Tansen directed.

She quivered, and her face pinched together as she tried to let the breath out in a slow, steady stream. The pressure became more and more uncomfortable until the last eight seconds, when she felt like she was suffocating. She couldn't control it any longer. Her remaining breath released like a noisy balloon deflating in one blast.

Tansen looked on with disappointment, and Seal watched as his face began to twitch strangely. *Is he going to burst out in rage? I know I failed horribly with that new exercise,* she worried. Then, suddenly, a great laugh shook his whole body. Sighing in relief, Seal smiled.

After his amusement had passed, he encouraged her, "Try again, try again."

Her teacher was very busy. There were days when Seal saw him only during her lesson, and he ushered her out quickly once it was over. Those times always left her feeling alone and a bit sad. However, in the evenings he would often come find her as she was finishing her work in the kitchen and ask her to walk with him. They would make their way across the mountain trails in the fading light of day. Despite his age and appearance, Tansen moved very quickly. Following behind, Seal would hear what sounded like a low chuckle, and suddenly he would pick up pace, forcing her to jog to keep up with him. One such time, when they returned to the monastery, Seal heard Tansen say to another monk, "I am very happy. Tonight, I have been hearing Seal behind me—*patta-patta-patta*—like a drum." He laughed.

Seal and Tansen also went on special outings together when it was time to buy food. His ancient eyes would sparkle as they ambled through the stalls at the open-air market. He selected brightly colored fruits and vegetables from the heaping piles displayed in bas-

kets and carts. Something about fresh, organic produce made him more excited than anything.

Once while selecting cucumbers, he took a big bite from one, wiggling it at her as he instructed, "It's of utmost importance to eat the freshest, healthiest food you can—every day. You are what you eat!" Little pieces of food flew from his mouth as he spoke excitedly. He ended by chomping off another big mouthful, then handed a cucumber to Seal, and they munched and crunched their way home.

Rarely, Seal got to accompany Tansen to a far-off temple when he traveled there to help with special services. He'd pull out an old silver scooter, and Seal would hop up behind him, sidesaddle. Then they would zoom off. She looked at his dear back as they rode along, staring at where his heart would be and feeling so much love and completeness just being there with him. His whiskers flapped back toward her face, and her fur blew around like crazy from the speed of the bike.

On one of these occasions, she felt that tingling in her brain again, like she had when she was a kitten. A feeling of deep peace flooded through every cell of her being. She wished they could just ride off into the sky and never come back. But eventually they arrived back at the monastery and life continued on.

The other temple was interesting. Seal enjoyed entering its dark, candlelit interior and happily watched as Tansen helped with the ceremony. The walls of the temple were covered with cloth-framed, colorful paintings that her teacher explained were called *thangkas.*

Some of the *thangkas* looked like angry monsters with fire around them. One showed a beautiful green person with hundreds of arms and several heads. Some others looked like Buddhas. Seal loved looking over all the various sacred images and wondered about their meanings. When he had time, Tansen told her about them.

"These are pictures of qualities that are inside every being. We all have Buddha-nature inside us," he said with reverence. "These paintings of peaceful Buddhas remind us of that."

"What about the green one with the many arms and heads?" Seal asked.

"That is a picture of Avalokiteshvara, who wanted to help heal the suffering of all beings and has so many arms and heads to help as many as possible," her teacher explained. "This reminds us we also have great compassion inside us for beings and creatures who are suffering."

"Oooh…" Seal breathed. Her eyes then darted to

one of the monsterlike images. "But what about that one? It looks angry!" She gestured toward a painting at the side of the room. In the center was a big circle that looked like a mandala. At the top, a fierce monster face was biting the circle with sharp-looking teeth. The creature's clawed hands and feet held the sides and bottom edges of the circle.

"That is the wheel of samsara. The circle represents the idea that if we live in a sleepwalking blindness, we'll go in vicious cycles that bring suffering to ourselves and others. The monster face at the top reminds us that everything is impermanent."

"Impermanent, like the sand mandala?"

"Exactly like the sand mandala!" He smiled. "Other parts in the center of the painting remind us that without awareness, our whole life can be like a hungry ghost who is never filled or satisfied, no matter what it receives."

Seal stared at the painting, her jaw hanging down. *I don't want my life to be like an endlessly hungry ghost or full of suffering!*

Tansen then directed her to one of the floor cushions before he began chanting with the other monks.

After the ceremony was over, he came to sit next to Seal, and they enjoyed the silence together. Eventually, the old cat looked at her and nodded, indicating that it was time to go. They got up and returned to the scooter, then began their windblown journey back to Tansen's monastery.

A day came when the monks were preparing to create a new sand mandala. Seal's eyes widened with surprise when Tansen handed her a set of tools. He loaded her cone with green sand and took her paws in his to show her how to vibrate a small stream of color onto the table.

Seal struggled to get the hang of it. Either she dumped out too much sand, or the stream got so thin it didn't cover the table properly. But the construction of the mandala took many hours over the next few weeks, and by the time it was completed, Seal's work was steady and precise. When the beautifully intricate mandala was completed, it was again destroyed. Seal couldn't help but feel a pang of sadness as the delicate, colorful image was swirled into nothingness.

Then one morning, some months after her arrival, she was finishing a hearty breakfast of spicy noodles and vegetables when Tansen asked her to join him for a walk in the garden. The air was crisp, and the sun was just piercing the cloud-dotted sky with shafts of gold. They walked together in silence for a while before he turned to her and spoke.

"Your time here is complete, Seal," he whispered, looking deep into her eyes.

Was that a faint tremor she heard in his voice? Her eyes filled with tears as she looked at her beloved teacher, then she followed his gaze out toward the garden. Mukti had arrived and was sitting on a rock in the sun. His eyes were closed, his spine straight, and he was perfectly still except for his beard. It flapped in the breeze, looking like it wanted to detach and fly away. Seal could see that the mouse was in the meditative space of quiet stillness Tansen had taught her.

"Remember what you have been taught, Seal." He

placed a loving paw on her shoulder and looked fixedly at her with his large, dark eyes. "When things seem the most difficult, silence, stillness, and the ability to slow your breath will help you. When you least want to sit, sit. It's most likely the best thing for you in those moments." He paused quietly as Seal looked up into his face. The corners of her mouth hung down in sadness. A smile crept across the old teacher's face as he added, "Mukti is taking you to a wise friend in Japan, where your studies will continue. Work hard, practice, and do your best."

So she was to continue learning, but not here. She imagined difficult things ahead and doubted her abilities. Even if her studies were successful, there was still the problem of how to find and save Ardaas. Seal slouched and her heart sank at the thought of being a disappointment to her teacher.

She had lived a small lifetime here at the temple. Her loving connection with Tansen was like a beautiful gift. She thought about the orphanage days and realized she could never have imagined having such a special master and loving friend. Tears pooled in her eyes and a sharp pain went through her heart as she struggled to speak. "I don't want to leave."

Tansen looked at her long and lovingly, then whispered, "Wait here a moment." She watched as he disappeared into the monastery, then returned with a large, dark bundle. "This is yours. You mastered it many lifetimes ago. Use it well."

Unwrapping the cloth, she found a strange wooden musical instrument with a bow inside. One end was sort of like a guitar, with a long neck, strings, and tuning pegs. But the other end was like nothing she had ever seen. It was shaped like a peacock. The rounded portion, where the sound came from, was the bird's body. It had a delicately carved neck and face, tiny feet came out of the bottom, and the back sported a plume of real, iridescent peacock feathers. Seal ran her paw over the smooth wood and gazed at it in awe. She had never seen anything so beautiful.

"What is it?" she whispered.

"It's your *taus*, Seal."

After carefully rewrapping the instrument, Tansen helped her sling it by a strap onto her back. She bowed to her teacher with humility and gratitude, and he bent over, enfolding her in a strong embrace. It felt like a jet stream of love pouring straight into her heart.

Mukti hopped down from his meditation spot to

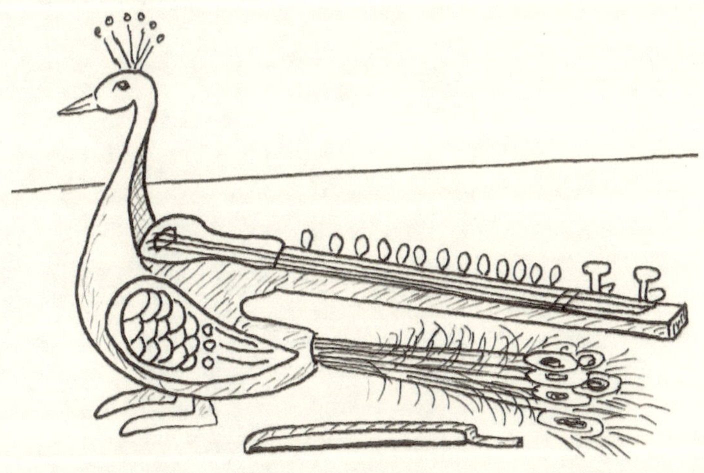

join her, and they both waved to Tansen before turning onto the path.

The tears in Seal's eyes could no longer be contained. Her cheeks grew wet as she walked. She didn't want Mukti to know she was upset. She didn't want to talk. Several times she looked over her shoulder, each time seeing Tansen's form in the garden, unmoving.

Mukti and Seal retraced the path to the open field, where the Cat Ship, in air-pressure mode, was descending from the heavens for boarding. They entered, ready to be transported to Japan.

CHAPTER 5

GHOSTS IN JAPAN

That evening, they landed in Tokyo and boarded a subway train.

"It's a two-hour ride to Chiba," Mukti informed her as he settled into his seat. The rocking of the car quickly lulled him into a deep slumber.

Seal eyed his beard again. *It looks so fake.* She couldn't resist leaning forward and reaching out. *One quick tug won't hurt,* she reasoned, *then I'll know if it's real or not.*

When her paw was millimeters away, Mukti's eyes snapped open, and he looked at her with sharp disapproval. Seal slowly moved backward as a guilty smile spread across her face.

It was nighttime when they reached their stop. Exiting the subway, they continued on foot. City gave way to village, then to semirural surroundings. Chestnut trees lined dusky lanes, which were flanked by tea-leaf bushes. A huge moon lit the landscape with its silver glow. Seal paused, admiring it.

The companions were delighting in the evening as they casually walked along. Gentle breezes caressed them, and the sweet scents of flowers and trees perfumed the air. However, the mood changed in a flash when they noticed something in the shadows up ahead. Pausing nervously, Seal and Mukti looked at each other, then back at the mysterious motion in the distance. A dark shape had detached from the landscape and was approaching them. It was a person.

"Why is it that passing a stranger at night feels scary and possibly dangerous?" Seal whispered to the mouse. She noticed that she had unconsciously picked up her pace, and Mukti was also scuttling faster alongside her. They were approaching an intersection ahead.

"Turn right when we get there," her bearded friend directed with anxiety in his voice.

Will we get there before the shadow person? Seal worried.

The pair zipped off to the right while the solitary traveler was still a good twenty paces away. Fearfully, Seal asked, "What should we do if the stranger follows us?"

Her companion ignored the question and remained silent.

Once they had gone fifteen paces up the new road, they turned to look back. The person was nearing the intersection.

"Keep going!" Mukti urged.

They sped up while still trying to keep to a walking pace—no sense making it obvious they were afraid or potentially trying to get away. After another fifteen steps, they peeked over their shoulders, then breathed huge sighs of relief. The mysterious shadow person had continued straight through the intersection. Seal smiled and Mukti chuckled in relief as their heartbeats and heaving chests returned to normal, then they continued on their way.

The companions moved on for some time without incident. Then a little further on, the lane disappeared into a dark, towering grove of bamboo. An instinctual warning made their fur stand on end.

"Anything could be hiding in there," Seal moaned. "We can't see more than a few steps ahead."

"Stay in the darkest shadows and move quickly," Mukti directed as they pattered down the deserted road.

"We're almost halfway through," Seal whispered hopefully.

Just as the moonlit path beyond the grove was becoming visible, a demonic red face burst forth from between the thick poles of bamboo. It had a nose like a sausage, an open mouth with metallic-looking teeth, and huge eyes. The creature let out what sounded like samurai warrior calls and lunged at them intimidatingly, using some form of martial art.

"Aghhhh!" Seal and Mukti screamed as they ran toward the open ground beyond the bamboo, hoping the creature would stay behind in the shadows.

But there, before them, was the red-faced demon. It had somehow beaten them to their retreat. Turning, they ran in the opposite direction. Again, the monster appeared out of nowhere, blocking their way. Its warrior calls were ferocious, and the leering red face looked ready to devour them. Once more, they began pumping their legs as fast as they could go, not stopping to look back. The straps of Seal's travel pack dug into her shoulders, and her *taus* was thumping painfully against her back as she ran. Speeding to the edge of a long rice field, they finally collapsed, out of breath.

Pricking up their ears, they listened but couldn't hear any sounds. The frightened pair stared back toward the sinister bamboo but couldn't see any sign of the demon. Then, turning forward, they froze. The creature's face was inches away from them, completely still and silent. Tilting its horrible face to the side, it surveyed them for several moments, then laughed.

The friends looked at each other in puzzlement—the monster's voice had changed. It now sounded light and cheerful. Seal and Mukti continued watching in suspense as two brown-and-black paws reached up and began removing the horrible red face. *It's a mask,* Seal realized in disbelief. Underneath was a small, wiry tiger-striped cat with green eyes that were so rounded and bright, they held a look of permanent surprise. A huge grin spread across its face.

"Mimi-chan," Mukti yelled out angrily, "you scared us to death!"

Seal relaxed, realizing there was no real danger. Apparently, Mukti knew this dramatic demon warrior/cat.

"Seal, this is your new teacher, Mimi-chan," he announced with irritation.

Doubt and concern filled Seal as she looked at the delicately framed striped cat.

Mimi-chan laughed, then turned to her. "You can call me Mi -chan. Come on, follow me!" she called out in a small, bell-like voice.

The three of them made their way back into the grove, then followed a narrow dirt pathway that emerged into a grassy clearing. The shadowy silhouettes of two buildings were visible beyond.

"Aisawa-san's ancestors have lived on this land for five hundred years," Mi-chan whispered with round eyes and awe in her voice. "They're even buried here!"

Seal's spine shivered, and she glanced down at

Mukti. He also seemed unsettled by the thought of ancient bodies in the ground beneath them.

Following Mi-chan through the darkness, they soon arrived at the smaller of the two buildings. "You can sleep here tonight," she said, rolling open a heavy door.

The building was an ancient, grass-roofed structure made of wood that was used to store harvested rice from the farm.

Mi-chan put her mask back on, then happily called out, "Good night!"

Seal and Mukti watched as she scampered off into the darkness, apparently to finish her night's work of haunting the bamboo grove.

The old building creaked as Seal entered. "Do you think there are ghosts in here, Mukti... Mukti?"

She turned around to see the mouse standing in the doorway, a look of horror in his little beady eyes. "Ghosts?" he whispered, his beard trembling.

Seal liked the way it felt to think of spooky things when there was no real threat. She hadn't realized Mukti would take the idea of ghosts so hard. "Come on, Mukti, lie down on these rice sacks."

He quickly scampered inside the folds, then peeked out fearfully.

Seal couldn't help wanting to have a little mischievous fun with him. "Close your eyes tight, just in case ghosts are flying around the ceiling!" She watched as his eyes pinched tightly shut and his body shuddered. Smiling, she decided to let the terrified mouse sleep.

They had experienced enough supernatural drama for one night.

Seal's body was tired, but her mind felt restless. Wandering out onto the porch, she sat watching fireflies as they floated over the grass and high into the trees. Unwrapping her *taus*, she admired it in the moonlight. Her paws went instinctively to the pegs and strings—*It feels like I know how to tune it*, she marveled. Next, she experimented with putting the bow to the strings in an attempt to play. All that came out was a terrible screech. Hissing in disgust, she hurriedly wrapped the *taus* back up, then placed it snugly in the corner.

Returning to the open doorway, Seal sat, becoming very still as the silence of night pooled around her. *I wonder what tomorrow will be like*, she mused as her eyelids began to droop heavily. Then the shock of an involuntary jerk made her realize she had fallen asleep.

Crawling over to the pile of rice sacks where Mukti was snoring away in high-pitched whistles, she curled up next to him and quickly fell into a deep slumber.

CHAPTER 6

AISAWA–SAN'S FARM

MORNING DAWNED. THE FIELDS OF THE FARM WERE moist with dew that reflected the rising sun.

Seal sat up and saw Mukti standing in the doorway, stretching and wiggling.

"What the heck are you doing?" she asked.

"Yoga," he panted as he continued without pause.

"Strange," Seal murmured as she studied his peculiar routine.

Mi-chan popped her head in the doorway just then. "Come up to the house for breakfast before you leave, Mukti."

Seal's face drooped in shock. "You're leaving?" she cried out. Mukti might be one strange mouse, but he was her friend. She realized she had really enjoyed his company. "Can't you stay just a little longer?" she pleaded.

"Let's go up to the house," was his only reply.

They walked slowly across the green lawn toward the large, old-fashioned farmhouse that stood prominently in the center. Seal had never seen anything like it with its grass roof and sliding doors. "Wow, this is amazing!" she whispered to the little bearded mouse as they slipped off their shoes in the entryway. Inside, the traditional Japanese flooring made of woven grass matting felt soft and cool under her paws. It smelled wonderfully fresh and sweet.

Aisawa-san stood across the room, turned away from them. He was a large tanuki. Seal knew that tanuki were special animals native to Japan and very rare to see. She had read all about them in her kitten days. Some people called them "raccoon dogs." Seal studied Aisawa-san. *A tanuki isn't really a raccoon and definitely not a dog. Tanuki are special unto themselves,* she decided.

The storybook at the orphanage had said that since ancient times, tanuki were thought to be magical and have many abilities, such as being able to transform into other objects. Seal remembered reading one story about a tanuki who had turned into a tea kettle and was only found out when it was placed over the fire and screamed. *A real, live tanuki!* She stared intently, wondering if he could shapeshift or had other magical powers.

Aisawa-san wore a Japanese *yukata* robe of indigo that was scattered with sky-blue starbursts. He turned to greet his visitors with a bow of the head. His long whiskers had a way of twirling around like parasols as he silently thought.

"Mimi-chan," he called out in a thick Japanese accent.

"Yes, Aisawa-san?"

"Please serve breakfast."

Aisawa-san bowed to Mukti and Seal with grace. He then walked over to a low, round table and gestured with his paw. "Please sit." There was an atmosphere of formality that was new for Seal. *I hope I don't accidentally embarrass myself!* she worried.

A small stack of cushions had been set out for Mukti so he could reach the tabletop easily. He climbed up and made himself ready. Seal watched Aisawa-san seat himself on his heels in the traditional posture on the grass flooring, and copied him.

Mi-chan brought out a tray of breakfast items. Seal and Mukti looked eagerly at the things placed before them. There was a savory broth with round white-and-pink swirled slices floating on top. On the side was a thick triangle wrapped in a layer of thin green seaweed. Seal bit into it and saw it was filled with delicious salty rice and had a sour plum hidden in the center. She liked the seaweed—it had a kind of fishy taste. Everything was so delicious.

Aisawa-san glanced over at her frequently but didn't say anything during the meal. When her dishes were empty, he quietly slid another tasty triangle onto her plate. She picked it up gently and slowly munched away, licking her paws when she was finished.

After they had eaten, Aisawa-san spoke again. "Seal, today you will work with Mimi-chan in the rice fields. We will meet again in the evening. Mukti, best of journey to you, dear friend." The mouse scampered over to him, and they bowed to each other, then hugged. "Come, I will walk you to the lane."

Mukti waved goodbye to Seal and Mi-chan, then left the house with Aisawa-san.

Seal assumed working in the rice fields would entail some sort of planting, weeding, or harvesting. She was quite surprised by the jobs she was given.

Before leaving the house, Mi-chan grabbed two large, thick canvas pouches, and they headed out onto the narrow earthen pathways that intersected the vast wet fields. Every now and then, they crossed over small bridges constructed from wooden planks. Occasionally, Seal glimpsed the movement of small frogs, which jumped away when she or Mi-chan got too close.

"The first task is spider relocation," Mi-chan announced, her eyes flashing with excitement.

Between two fig trees on the edge of the field was a massive web. In the center, a huge black-and-yellow spider clung in stillness, awaiting its next meal. Looking around, Seal noticed that many such webs could be seen between trees bordering the fields. Mi-chan quickly swiped the spider from its perch and into her pouch. Seal was reluctant. The giant arachnids looked scary with their long legs and multiple eyes.

"Come on, hurry," her teacher prompted.

Seal gave it a go but moved too slowly. The sticky webbing caught on her paw along with the spider, which started crawling up her arm. "Aaaaagh!" she screamed as it moved toward her face.

Mi-chan laughed, then swatted the spider gently into her own pouch. "Quick action, Seal!"

She tried again, and this time her reflexes were better. They continued on until their pouches were full.

Mi-chan guided the way to an unused corner of the farm, where they emptied the critters out. Seal cringed at the sight of all those spiders wriggling in a pile.

Next was the work of keeping the crow, Karasu-san, and his family away from the rice seedlings. After stowing their spider pouches, Mi-chan opened a cupboard and removed two red tengu masks that looked like the one she'd worn the night before.

"Tengu is a protector of the forest. The masks are useful for crop protection as well as night-watch security," she explained with a wink.

They put the masks on, and as they were heading out, Seal caught her eerie reflection in a mirror. A shudder passed through her at the scary face looking back with her own eyes behind it.

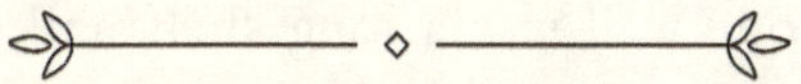

The two cats spent several hours out in the fields, crawling, jumping, and using samurai warrior cries to startle Karasu-san and his family up into the sky.

Seal noticed Aisawa-san in an adjacent field, tending to young fruit trees. He paused now and then, apparently watching their routine.

Looking over at Mi-chan popping up and down while shouting, she smiled. Her new teacher's slim cat body paired with the fierce red face was quite a sight. Seal laughed, knowing she looked just as strange.

The sun was sinking low on the horizon as the exhausted workers returned to the house.

"I hope we'll start dinner soon," Seal pantingly said to Mi-chan. "I'm starving!" But as soon as they had removed their shoes and stowed the masks, they heard Aisawa-san's voice calling out.

"Seal, come with me to the tatami room," he ordered.

Disappointment filled her as she realized her aching stomach was going to have to wait.

They entered the large room, where a sweet breeze was flowing through the outer doorway. Settling down on the grass-mat flooring, they crossed their legs and straightened their spines.

Aisawa-san closed his eyes and was silent for a long time.

Seal watched him for a few moments, then her attention wandered. She looked over the sitting room. The walls and ceiling were covered in beautiful dark wood. On one wall was a long shelf and, below that, a niche, which held an incense burner, a small vase of

flowers, and some other objects that reminded Seal of things she had seen in the temple with Tansen.

I wonder what the training here will be like, she mused. After a while, she glanced back at the tanuki and saw that he was watching her steadily, under mostly closed eyelids. Her body jolted. *What if he can read my thoughts?* She gulped, then gave him her full attention.

"You learned many things from your time with Tansen, yes?" Aisawa-san inquired.

Seal nodded, recalling her beautiful time at the temple and her teacher's parting gift of the *taus*.

"It is important to keep up your practice of sitting quietly and not grabbing on to your thoughts," Aisawa-san said. "Let's practice together now." He adjusted his robes, then closed his eyes.

Seal closed her eyes and became still.

"Relax," he reminded her.

Realizing she had been tensing her shoulders and tail she let them soften. Focusing her attention, she became aware of the subtle things in her surroundings. The house was creaking slightly, the air smelled of blossoms, and a fly was lazily buzzing around the room. After some time, she heard a thumping sound. Puzzled, she began listening more intently. *It's my own heartbeat!* she noticed in surprise. Then Seal observed the spaces between beats as they grew longer and longer.

At some point the beats disappeared into complete silence. Then the silence started to seem strangely loud to her. It had a roaring quality. Listening, she breathed, long and deep. Time disappeared.

Aisawa-san cleared his throat, and she snapped back to the present moment, opening her eyes. The sun had long since set, and the moon was now climbing in the sky. *How long have we been sitting? It must have been more than an hour.* Seal was puzzled, but she also felt a glowing joy. Some part of that wonderful magic feeling she'd experienced as a kitten had returned.

"We'll sit together in the evenings while you're here," Aisawa-san remarked as he rose and stretched. By now, hunger was gnawing at everyone.

"Come help me in the kitchen." Mi-chan directed.

I want to share something with my new teachers, Seal decided. Rummaging through her travel bag, she found a tiny bag of dried rice. It was all she had to offer.

While Mi-chan was delicately preparing various vegetables, Seal began boiling water. She poured in the sparse grains and watched them floating around the large pot as she stirred with her paddle. It didn't look like it would feed even one of them. Seal said a sincere

little prayer, hoping somehow it would be enough, then covered the pot with a heavy lid.

Aisawa-san and Mi-chan placed beautifully painted blue-and-white dishes of different sizes on the red table. Larger bowls held a wonderful-looking soup made with lacy lotus root, daikon, burdock, mushrooms, and potatoes. Smaller dishes were heaped with seaweed salad. When the time was just right, Seal brought the rice pot to the table and kneeled down with her companions. They blessed the meal in the traditional Japanese way, chanting, "Itadakimasu!"

Then the tanuki paused, staring at the rice pot intently before removing the lid with a flourish of gusto and letting out a samurai-like call, "Urrrrrr ahh!" Seal gasped; the rice had swollen and multiplied beyond belief.

As they ate, Aisawa-san told Seal about his family. "This farmhouse was built by my great-grandfather. But our family has lived on this land for many hundreds of years." He pointed to a carving of his family shield. "It has figs on it, which are good to eat. My neighbor's shield has arrows on it—not good to eat." He chuckled.

When the meal was finished, Seal and Mi-chan cleared the table while Aisawa-san set up his art supplies and began working on a beautiful landscape painting. Seal watched, intrigued.

As his brush masterfully created mountains, sky, and fields, he spoke to her. "You are here to work and learn. Tomorrow you must begin learning." Aisawa-san gave a knowing look to Mi-chan, who stopped cleaning her paws and gave a nod of assent.

What will I be learning? Seal wondered with intense curiosity.

CHAPTER 7

SOTO TECHNIQUE

THE NEXT DAY, SEAL WOKE TO MI-CHAN PULLING OFF her blanket. "Wake up, Seal. It's time to start!"

Opening her eyes halfway, she saw it was still dark and curled up tighter.

"Come on!" her feisty new teacher called out before playfully biting Seal's tail.

"Ow!" Seal shot up, giving her undivided attention.

"First order of the day is exercise. Follow me."

Seal watched as Mi-chan began a series of movements coordinated with her breath. It was a lot like what she had seen Mukti doing before. "Inhale, twist left, exhale, twist right," the small, wiry cat directed.

Seal twisted and puffed in and out. The stretching and breathing made her feel good. But then came a very difficult exercise.

"Lie flat on your back and lift your back feet just a bit into the air. Like this." Mi-chan demonstrated.

Seal tried, but her whole body started to shake uncontrollably.

"Keep trying, Seal! Breathe!"

"Why…are…we…doing this?" Seal strained to speak. She was still trembling, and her brow had broken out in sweat.

"Yoga…strengthens your…nervous system…and keeps you…flexible," Mi-chan puffed out as she fought to keep her feet up.

Seal couldn't take it any longer. She let out a sigh and collapsed to the floor limply.

Mi-chan held her posture a few seconds longer, then gracefully released her feet down on an exhale. Seal gazed sideways at her in disbelief.

Then both cats sat up and stretched their arms and legs wide, breathing deeply. That was followed by forward, backward, and side bending. They lay down on the floor, this time on their bellies, in what Mi-chan called "cobra pose." This position felt much more natural to Seal. She pushed up with her front paws, lifting her chest and chin to the sky and stretching the length of her spine in a very catlike arch.

"Next is chair pose," Mi-chan directed. She showed Seal how to crouch low on her haunches without touching the ground, as if there were a chair under her.

It was challenging, and Seal started to tremble again.

"One last posture," Mi-chan called out. "Camel pose."

Seal watched as her instructor came onto her haunches, then arched backward, grabbing her back paws. She looked like a sort of furry doughnut, and Seal couldn't hold back a giggle. The posture looked difficult, but Seal found that her feline spine bent into the new shape very easily.

They remained there a couple minutes, breathing long and deep.

"And…release!"

The two cats unfurled themselves and breathed normally.

"Now, to prepare for meditation," Mi-chan continued, "sit with pretzel legs and your back straight. Squeeze and release the muscles along your spine, up and down."

It took Seal a while to feel where those muscles were, let alone flex them.

The pair sat in silence while their breathing slowed and deepened.

Seal felt a big train of thoughts coming through. She noticed she was grabbing many of them, and a knot was growing in her stomach. The deep silence wasn't coming. Her body ached, and it felt like she had been sitting for hours. Feeling restless, she started to fidget.

When Mi-chan finally rang a tiny bell, Seal sighed in relief. "How long did we meditate? Was it three hours?"

Mi-chan laughed and replied, "It was only twenty minutes!"

"Why didn't the time go fast like last night?" Seal asked, disappointed.

Aisawa-san appeared just then and replied in his beautiful accent, "Every experience is unique—like a snowflake. Appreciate each one as it is. The time you spend in silence is valuable, even when it feels difficult."

Seal sighed. *Well, I guess it won't hurt to keep it up, then.*

After breakfast, Mi-chan took Seal to the bamboo grove. "Now we're going to study an ancient art called soto technique—secret walking. It's an ancient form of movement that allows you to infiltrate any opponent's lair silently. It also gives you fast moves so you can escape dangerous situations," she informed her. "You need some skills if you are going to face Kadir and try to get Ardaas away from him. Soto technique is just the thing."

Seal thought about Mi-chan's words for a moment. *I've been so busy learning and living. I haven't even considered how I might find and save Ardaas.* Her friend from time before time seemed like a far-off dream, not a real soul in danger. Her heart held many different emotions. *Part of me just wants to forget about Ardaas and keep living on the farm or go back to Tansen's monastery.*

Then she remembered the past-life visions of her time with her friend. There was a reality to them that gave her the determination to move ahead with what lay before her. *Ardaas needs my help. From what Tansen said, his life depends upon me. I can't ignore that. I'll do my best to learn whatever is necessary to complete this journey,* she decided.

Hours went by as Mi-chan instructed Seal on various sequences of paw positions, balancing, jumping, lunging, and spinning techniques—all designed to help her traverse long distances and varied terrain in complete silence. Seal did passably well in grass and dirt

but failed terribly when Mi-chan challenged her with a creaky wooden floor and gravel pathways scattered with obstacles. She became discouraged.

"You can't master it all in one lesson." Mi-chan placed a loving paw on Seal's shoulder.

They called it a day and went back to the farmhouse for dinner.

Seal settled into a daily routine with her studies and made great progress over the next several months.

Most of the time, she enjoyed the various morning yoga sets. Sometimes Mi-chan would throw a new exercise at her that felt impossible and left her shaking and breathless.

Sometimes, meditation time with Mi-chan and Aisawa-san felt fast and deep, and other times, it was like an impossible struggle that lasted an eternity. But

Seal remembered not to worry about it and just kept going. Her lessons with Mi-chan were coming along, and she was improving with her *taus*.

Late one hot afternoon, she was practicing soto technique in the treacherous gravel- and litter-strewn areas. Mi-chan had scattered sharp tacks here and there to make her more alert and also to see if she could keep quiet if she accidentally stepped on them. Seal had been practicing for many hours already and was drenched with sweat and limp with fatigue. "I still can't clear the difficult areas silently," she complained.

"One more time, Seal. Then you can go inside for the night," the slim cat ordered.

She began again, but only a quarter of the way in, her paw hit a tack with her full weight. Pain shot up her leg and she cried out in agony and frustration.

"I don't want to keep doing this! I'm no good at it. I keep making the same mistakes." Hobbling off, she added, "Maybe Ardaas doesn't even exist. Why should I work so hard for something that might not even be real?"

Mi-chan stared blankly at her. Then the sound of Aisawa-san clearing his throat made them both jump. He had been screened behind a large ornamental tree that he was silently pruning.

Seal looked down, embarrassed that the tanuki had witnessed her outburst.

"Seal, follow me." His voice was firm and direct.

Her head sank as she hurried behind him toward the house.

Aisawa-san sat at his worktable and motioned for Seal to come beside him. He pulled out a fresh sheet of paper, an inkpot, and a soft brush. With one quick, elegant movement, he shifted his sleeve up and began rendering an image with the fat brush and deep-black ink. It soon took on terrifying features. When he was finished, the tanuki pulled Seal directly in front of the finished picture.

Staring up at her, much too lifelike, was an image of the scarred ape, Kadir. He looked powerful and dark. His eyes were filled with anger and hatred, his hair matted and filthy. A permanent scowl was carved into his brow. The mouth was slightly open, showing large teeth and a chipped left incisor. Penetrating and cold, there was no love or compassion in the features. The image was so vivid that a stench from the gorilla seemed to enter the room. Seal tried to pull away from the table. She wanted to run and never see that terrible face again, but Aisawa-san held her there.

"This is what you must face." He spoke urgently.

"Ardaas is in his possession. He will kill him." He paused, then continued gently, "Only you can find him. You have the soul connection."

Seal stared at the image, frightened. Pulling back with more force, she finally broke free and bolted out the door. She didn't know where to go—she just ran, a flash of white and gray against the landscape.

Zipping through deserted lanes, Seal fled across fields toward a nearby hill. The fading daylight revealed moss-covered steps bordered by thick trees snaking up the hillside. Branches formed a canopy overhead, making a living tunnel.

She sped upward, not pausing until she arrived at the top. Seal found herself in a small clearing, shaded from all sides by large, ancient trees.

Allowing her breath to return to normal, she sat gazing at the landscape and listened to the crickets and voices of the pines as the wind combed through their branches. The moon was rising, and it cast a bluish glow down through the upstretched arms of the giant trees.

The terrible image of Kadir was burning in her mind. She focused deeper into silence. She didn't know how much time had passed, but after a while, the faint sound of a bell pierced the air from far in the distance. It awoke something within her. She felt a flush of sensation rise in her body, from her tail to the crown of her head. Then her attention became fixed as memories began to appear in the darkness of her mind. The past was again coming alive...

Ardaas in his cat body—orange, cream, and fluffy.

She saw herself with him in a boat. *We must have been living in Japan. We're wearing patterned* yukata *robes.* Sunlight was glinting brightly on splashing blue waves, and they were laughing. The boat was moving quickly down a river.

Suddenly, as they rounded a bend, sharp currents began to tumble the small vessel violently. They couldn't control it, and Seal was thrown off. She saw her limp shape sinking down through the deep, heavy water. The fast-moving waves churned and sucked her toward the bottom. Bubbles of air escaped from her nose and mouth. She gasped, and water began pouring into her.

Then, she felt strong claws digging into her body, followed by the sensation of moving upward. It was Ardaas. Near the surface, he grabbed her neck scruff tightly in his teeth and dragged her to the shore, where they both lay collapsed from weakness.

Seal's large blue eyes popped open. The vision faded into the darkness of the forest. She shivered, and her heart was pounding. *Ardaas saved* me. *I have to save him!*

For a long time, she sat in silence among the whispering trees as the cicadas began to sing. Then, with a peaceful determination, she began the walk back to the farm.

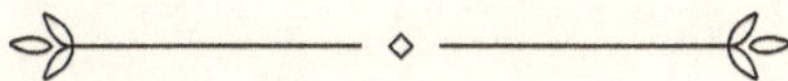

The next morning over breakfast, Aisawa-san gazed steadily at her, then asked, "What do you believe about this Universe, Seal?"

She mused for a moment as she chewed her seaweed triangle. "That it's confusing and difficult," she said as she looked across the table. "What do you believe about the Universe, Aisawa-san?"

As he looked at her, his whiskers twisted in each direction. "I believe in the ways of Shinto, that a Divine force is in all things. In the rocks, trees, water… the mountain, sunshine, all creatures and beings…everything. You could say it another way too—God is in all things."

Seal pondered his words as she took in the landscape of the farm through the open doorway. The sky was dawning with purple-blue clouds. Dragonflies had begun soaring like miniature airplanes over the dewy grass. Aisawa-san's voice echoed in her mind. *"Divine force is in all things."* She didn't know anything about Shinto, but she felt deep truth in those words.

After breakfast, Mi-chan took Seal outside, where they resumed her lessons. This time, Seal kept seeing

the vision of Ardaas from the night before in her mind. She felt motivated to try harder than ever before. She owed it to her friend.

She practiced the moves until they were smooth. Then, later in the day, the big test came—the gravel patch. Mi-chan sprinkled extra tacks on the ground and added several more obstacles. After arranging the new course, she moved off to the side to watch.

Glancing over, Seal noticed that Aisawa-san was secretly observing behind a screen of trees. "Mi-chan?"

"Yes?"

"Why do we have to leave the big test for after I've been practicing all day for hours?" She sighed with fatigue. "Why not when I am rested and fresh?"

"Because," Mi-chan answered confidently, "if you can do it now, we'll know you can do it even better when you're not tired." She answered with a wink.

Sulking in defeat, she sighed, knowing what her teacher had said was true.

Seal's exhaustion was making her lose her grip. Her body was trembling from all the hours of practice. "Ardaas saved me. I want to repay him," she whispered under her breath. Narrowing her eyes, she steadied herself and began. A third of the way through the course, she paused, trying to keep herself from collapsing in fatigue. She caught her breath, then continued. Leap, crawl, pause—turn, glide, soar. She landed with a small thud on the soft earth at the end of the course. She had done it!

"You need to work on your final landing, but otherwise, not bad." Mi-chan grinned.

Seal offered a weak smile back, panting. Then she looked toward the trees, but Aisawa-san was gone.

After supper, Seal curled up in a circle on the sweet-grass floor to rest her weary body. The tip of her tail twitched as she looked out the doorway. Fireflies flickered their lantern bodies as they traveled around the farm.

"A message arrived from Mukti this morning," Aisawa-san announced. "Kadir is in the vicinity of Koyasan, the holy mountain and burial ground. Ardaas is most likely with him. Tomorrow you must leave early."

Seal was shocked by this news. She was sure she wasn't ready to encounter that scarred ape. How could she possibly succeed? She also felt pangs of homesickness even though she hadn't left yet. The farm had become dear to her. Aisawa-san and Mi-chan were her family as well as her teachers. Couldn't she stay longer, practicing until she was *really* prepared for what lay ahead?

Aisawa-san looked up from his painting. "Let us hear your progress." He gestured with his paintbrush toward the corner where her *taus* was leaning against the wall. Then he continued to focus on his work.

She had been practicing, but it was still challenging. Now and then, her bow would call forth a voice of ancient beauty. Many other times, it made sounds no one wanted to hear.

Taking up her *taus*, she returned to the open doorway to be cooled by the evening air as she played. Steadying her breath, she readied her bow and began.

A sorrowful melody floated upon the air, circling the room, rising and falling before fading out. Seal gently lifted the bow from the strings, then cradled her *taus* lovingly.

Looking up, she saw the tanuki had frozen from his work, brush in hand. He was looking at her directly with his dark brown eyes. Were those tears glistening in the corners? His stare made her feel shy, and she looked down at the floor timidly. Aisawa-san quietly put away his painting tools, then began gathering supplies for her journey. She watched as he took her embroidered pouch and filled it with rice crackers and dried figs from the farm.

"Be vigilant on Koyasan," he said, looking at her with concern. "Besides Kadir, there are terrible mosquitoes and *hiru*."

"What are *hiru*?" she asked.

"I cannot think of the English translation." Aisawa-san paused in thought. "Perhaps…slug?"

Seal was mystified. Why should she worry about a slug?

Mi-chan brought her a polished blue agate amulet. "It's the color of your eyes. It's your third eye!" She smiled as she handed it to Seal, who trilled with delight as she slipped the thin cord around her neck. It felt like a magical gift.

"Mount Koyasan is not on the Cat Ship's route. You will take the subway to the central station tomorrow," Aisawa-san directed, "then continue on the main train line." He handed her coins for the subway and a thin paper train ticket stamped with the destination, *Koyasan.*

That night she lay, staring with wide eyes into the complete darkness of the room. Her heart ached at the thought of leaving, and her mind was troubled. *How can I possibly find Ardaas when I don't know what he looks like anymore? And Kadir...* She shivered as she recalled Aisawa-san's depiction. She had no words for the fear and anxiety that overwhelmed her when thinking of confronting that savage gorilla.

Dawn arrived all too soon. Seal breakfasted with her Japanese teachers one last time, then said a sad goodbye before walking to the subway station. *Will I ever see Aisawa-san, Mi-chan, or the wonderful farm ever again?* She wondered tearfully as each step took her farther away.

CHAPTER 8

KOYASAN

SEAL HANDED HER TICKET TO THE TRAINMASTER, THEN boarded with her travel bag and *taus*. She would arrive at the base of the mountain in about seven hours.

The landscape whizzed by, and her eyelids began to hang as she floated in and out of consciousness.

Eyes opened, city changed to town, eyes closed. Eyes opened, town changed to village, eyes closed. Eyes opened, village changed to bamboo-covered mountains with thick mists in their folds.

Seal was the only passenger still onboard when the train reached the end of the line. It was now late afternoon. Stepping onto the platform, she crossed over to board a steeply angular cable car that would take her to the top of the mountain, where a village of monasteries and the cemetery was nestled. Her stomach began to ache. She wasn't sure if it was hunger or fear of what was to come.

A five-minute ride brought her to the top, where she exited. A little way off stood two curious figures in saffron robes, one with a hood. The hooded figure was a very round tanuki with black fur and dark, sleepy eyes. The other one was a thin red fox with a cream-colored neck and strange yellow eyes that had pupils like a cat's. Seal went toward them.

"I'm Ensho," the fox said in a soft voice, "and this is Gyoki." He gestured to his portly companion. "Come with us," he said, then he turned and started up the mountain road.

There was no one else there. Seal figured she'd better follow. No other words passed between them as their foot journey continued. *Maybe every stranger visiting the mountain is greeted this way,* she mused as she walked leisurely alongside her silent guides.

They walked for a long time up the curving road. The mountain vibrated with the life of thousands of ancient trees. Here and there, monastery gates ap-

peared among the greenery, and various temples could be seen behind them. Ferns, moss, and little tufts of plants popped up everywhere.

Eventually, they turned into one of the tall wooden gateways. It was beautifully ornamented with a traditional twisted *shimenawa* rope, hanging in a swag from the top and decorated with zigzag shaped white paper prayer flags. *It feels so magical!* Seal thought as she paused to look up, her mouth gaping in awe.

Inside the courtyard were several ancient trees with massive trunks. Some of these also had *shimenawa* tied around them, like belts, with more prayer flags hanging off the ropes. *It looks like a blessing for the trees,* she thought with a smile.

The three companions paused in the entry hall. It was a square room that had a wall lined with shelves just for holding shoes. Seal noticed the monks had high wooden sandals, just like the ones she and Ardaas wore in one of her past-life memories.

After removing their shoes, they continued down a highly polished wooden hallway that made Seal's furry paws slide.

As they moved past an open doorway leading to an inner courtyard, Seal paused to look out. It was a picturesque scene containing an ornamental garden and pond with Japanese maple trees overhanging the edges of the water. Small green frogs, with surprisingly loud voices, were crooning. After a few moments, she reluctantly turned away and hurried to rejoin her guides.

They entered a large hall where a sea of robed monks were seated in meditation. Ensho directed her to sit, then he and Gyoki joined her.

Seal tried to come into stillness, but her mind was unruly. Thoughts were bombarding her like missiles. Many of them were troublesome worries about the future and others were curious wonderings about this strange, interesting place. It felt like an eternity before the monks finally stirred and began departing.

The fox and chubby tanuki then guided her to the other end of the monastery, where the dormitory was located. She was shown up a low flight of steps and down a hallway. Ensho slid a door open, revealing a large room. It contained a futon mattress on the floor, covered with a thick quilt, and a water basin with pitcher. A small lamp lit the space, and in the center of the floor sat two small tables. They had been lain out with a supper. The room's delicate walls were made of paper, painted with wonderful designs of flowers, trees, and animals. The panels could be slid open or closed to join or separate rooms as needed.

"Seal," the fox said in low, gentle tones, "tomorrow you must wake early to help with the fire ceremony. Please come to the hall across from the garden promptly at six."

A startled jolt passed through Seal as Ensho spoke. *They know my name! Aisawa-san and Tansen must know them,* she decided. She nodded, then watched the two figures depart. How far away her time with Tansen seemed now.

Carefully, she placed her gear in a corner, then sat down and began devouring the delicious food. When she was finished eating, she explored the room. One of the wall panels had a stylized tiger with crossed eyes, which made it look part demon. Seal imitated the look on the tiger's face, then broke down laughing. A traditional cotton *yukata* robe lay folded up on the futon for her to use. It had a delicate pattern of luna moths scattered over it. Slipping into the roomy sleeves, she wrapped the front, tying it snugly.

Seal curled up on the futon, watching the shadows lengthen as the blue tones of evening filled the room. Her body was exhausted, but sleep would not come. Soon she was tossing and turning as her mind grabbed ahold of many unpleasant thoughts and feelings. With a great sigh, she tried to let the thought train pass on, bringing herself back to the present moment.

Her ears perked up as the silence was broken by sounds of monks entering the adjoining chambers. It sounded like Gyoki, the portly tanuki, was in the room to her left. The monastery gradually returned to silence, and the building itself seemed to sigh into sleep.

Seal continued listening in the darkness as the sounds of cicadas, frogs, and other strange, small creatures floated in through the open window.

After what felt like hours, she got up and switched on the lamp. Scanning the room, she pondered, *What can I do?* Her eyes fell on her travel bag, *Some organizing might be helpful.*

She began to rifle through it, pulling out plastic bags that rattled noisily before she came to the pouch that contained the polished amulet Mi-chan had given her. *My third eye,* she thought as she held it up over her nose. She trilled as she viewed it with crossed eyes. The lamplight illuminated the semitransparent stone, and her focus locked. She felt as if a beam of energy was coming out of her brow flame with the strength of a laser. Holding her focus, she went deeper. A peaceful calm came over her in waves, and she began to see a vision.

In a sky of bluish-green light, a delicate, iridescent hummingbird was suspended in the air. It buzzed around joyously from flower to flower, feeding and enjoying the warmth of the sun. Such a tiny creature would bring joy to anyone who saw it. Suddenly, a heavy, dark net crashed down over the delicate bird, entrapping it. *What does it mean?* Seal wondered.

The lamp flickered off, Seal's focus snapped, and the stone fell to the floor with a loud *thunk.* As she scrambled around for it in the darkness, she became caught in the plastic bags, causing a terrible racket as she tried to free herself.

An alarming bang sounded as the door to her room forcefully slid open.

Seal froze, and the lamp flickered back to life.

Gyoki stood in the doorway. An angry look was flashing in his eyes. "This is much noise!" he gruffly whispered. "Can you not sleep?"

In an instant, she realized that every sound she'd made had traveled through the paper walls as easily as if they hadn't been there. Gulping, she looked up at the chubby tanuki from her plastic trap, then shook her head.

"Please follow instructions for ancient sleeping technique, or I will be forced to tie you up!" There weren't many hours between bedtime and the fire ceremony each morning, and apparently her commotion had worn Gyoki's patience to its end.

Cringing with embarrassment, she continued rustling around to free herself. As she rose to walk forward, a loud crinkling sound made her look down. One of the bags was still attached to her back paw. Energetically, she flicked the foot one final time, then watched the offending plastic float off to the side.

The large tanuki let out a frustrated grunt as she sheepishly gazed at him. With heavy steps, he trudged over to the large blue-and-white porcelain pitcher and poured some water into the basin. "Put feet in there— all of them," he ordered.

Seal jumped into the bowl. *It's so icy!* She felt her eyes bulge and her fur stand on end. *This feels colder than any winter I can remember.*

"Stay!" Gyoki raised a paw.

Seal shivered violently. "Do I have to stay in?" she said through chattering teeth. "This water must have run off some high, snowy mountain." After several minutes, her body began to relax, and after another few minutes, she was surprised to realize that she was beginning to feel pleasantly warm. It was soothing.

"Slowly come out." The tanuki directed, the anger now gone from his voice.

Out she climbed.

"Lie down," he directed.

Seal started to curl up on her left side, like usual.

"No, no, right side only, please," he insisted.

She adjusted herself.

"Now, most important final step. Please use right paw. Plug right side of nose."

Seal began raising the specified paw but paused midair. *How can all this crazy stuff make you sleep?* she thought as she gave Gyoki a sidelong glance.

His brow furrowed, and his eyes darkened at her hesitation.

Like a flash, she fulfilled his command, not wanting to irritate the large tanuki further.

"Cover right side, breathe deep. Begin!" he whispered with the force of a shout.

This is ridiculous, she thought as she continued following his orders.

After several breaths, she realized her paw had somehow slipped down. Lifting it back up to cover the right side of her nose, she continued breathing, but it slipped again.

The room grew dim, then disappeared.

The next thing she knew, she was being startled awake by the clanging morning bell.

"Huh, it worked," she whispered to herself. Jumping to her feet, she adjusted her robe, then made her way down the dark hallway.

Reaching the sacred ceremony chamber, she slid open the heavy door and slipped inside.

CHAPTER 9

THE INARI SHRINE

SEAL WAS JUST IN TIME FOR THE FIRE CEREMONY.
The dim hall looked like a mystical, glowing forest. A sort of metal canopy that reminded her of leaves hung suspended from the ceiling, and groups of long ribbons cascaded down on the sides. Seal thought they looked like massive trunks. The canopy shimmered and danced in the firelight.

Saffron-robed monks were spread throughout the chamber in uneven clusters. Most of them were seated on the right side of the room. Already, their deep voices were beginning to stir the silence with the chanting of ancient, sacred prayers. To the left, Ensho was seated on a platform where a decent-sized fire was crackling. He periodically placed long, flat sticks inscribed with prayers into the flames. The open space in front of the monks was filled with residents from the village who had come to observe.

Seal was directed to walk the perimeter of the ceremonial area where the monks were sitting. Just as she neared the fire, Ensho added a stick, making it flare. It singed her tail, and she picked up her pace, scrambling out of the flames' reach. Continuing around, she was handed an offering of tea leaves, which she placed with reverence on an altar at the far side of the room, behind all the rows of monks. She continued around the aisle, then sat in the very back with the villagers on the floor. Seal was enjoying the feeling of being in a golden forest. Occasionally, she narrowed her eyes as she went into a very deep space of inner stillness. The monks continued chanting, and one by one, the prayer sticks were consumed by the fire.

Afterward, breakfast was served. She was directed to a small chamber overlooking the pond, where a handful of monks were having tea. As she sat down, she was handed a small jade-colored porcelain cup shaped like a lotus blossom. Her nose twitched pleasantly as it took in the fragrance of jasmine wafting up from the steaming cup.

Just then, Ensho looked toward her and began speaking in his soft voice. "Kadir and Ardaas are believed to be hidden in the shady forests of Okunoin— the largest cemetery in all of Japan. You must set out soon."

Seal fidgeted. Again, the pressure and responsibility of her mission began to weigh heavily upon her.

"Gyoki," the fox continued, "which route is best for Seal?"

The tanuki mulled this over for a long time, munching his muzzle before answering. "From west."

Ensho studied Seal, then nodded. "More information to help your journey is expected to arrive some-time today. When we receive it, you can set out. We don't know when you will return," he added in a serious tone that dropped off into silence.

Seal gulped and slumped down as she remembered the image of Kadir, etched in her mind.

Ensho, seeming to sense her discomfort then continued, "Finish your breakfast, then go out and enjoy some sunshine and fresh air. You must leave soon enough."

Seal tried to enjoy the beautiful food she was served. A dozen small bowls of different shapes were brought to her on a small-legged tray that doubled as a table. The aromas made her mouth water. She didn't recognize any of the foods, but she wasn't afraid to try them. Some things were sweet, some surprised her by puckering her mouth with sourness, and some things, like the long, fried vegetable pieces, were salty. It was all so delicious.

After breakfast, Gyoki gave her some money and sacks. "Ensho wants you to buy oranges. They are for spiritual offerings. Also choose some for your journey."

She looked at the coins in her paw. Some had circular holes in the center that she could peek through. "I'm going to bring my *taus* with me," she said, sliding the money into her pouch. "It might help keep my mind from worrying."

She quickly gathered her things, then the tanuki walked her to the gate.

"This way to the market." He gestured to the left.

Koyasan was beautiful beyond words. The cold,

damp morning air smelled of ancient trees, ferns, and moss growing in profusion. Seal padded along the road, marveling at the lush greenery as she made her way up the curving road, which, after some time, broadened into a small plaza. Across the way, she could see a man with a cart selling small, bright oranges and bundles of glossy, dark green leaves, which were also used as offerings. She filled the large sack for the monastery and chose a few juicy-looking fruits to add to the small sack that would be traveling with her.

As she retraced her route, she noticed something she hadn't seen on the way up. Between a building and a large bush was a narrow dirt pathway leading upward. Taking a few steps inside and passing beyond the snagging arms of the bush, she marveled as the space opened out into a stone-lined path that was arched over by dozens of scarlet-and-black torii gates. It looked so interesting and inviting. Seal felt drawn to explore it, so up she went.

At the top was a large grassy clearing. Everything was silent, not a soul to be seen. On the far side, nestled in dense forest, a solitary red torii gate stood just before the doorway of a weathered wooden structure that looked like a gate house to something beyond.

Seal glanced around. *I wonder if anyone is watching me.* She carefully trotted across the grass and disappeared inside the gate house.

Red and white ribbons and a massive rope with a huge tassel at the bottom hung down from the ceiling. On the opposite wall, another doorway led outside

again. Other than the things hanging from the ceiling, the gate house was empty and dark.

Seal crept forward, curious to see what lay outside the second doorway.

One final red-and-black torii gate stood in front of a small house-like shrine with an elegantly curved roof. Several massive trees grew in a circle surrounding the shrine, and two stone fox statues flanked either side. They looked regal with their long, knowing eyes and red cloth bibs that had been tied on them as a blessing. The space had a magical feeling about it, hidden away from the world and containing such beauty.

Seal trilled with joy. She recognized that this was a Shinto shrine dedicated to the fox god called Inari Okami. Aisawa-san had taught her some things about Shinto while she was at his farm. The little shrine building nestled in the trees was made to be a home for the god or kami. He had also taught her how to pray at Shinto shrines. "Bow twice, then clap twice," he had instructed, then demonstrated with two reverent bows and two firm, loud claps. "The clapping is so you get the god's attention," he whispered. Then, in his normal tone, he continued, "Next, you pray and bow one final time. Now, show me, so I know you have learned properly and will remember."

Seal did remember, and the tanuki would have been pleased if he'd seen how reverently she bowed and clapped now before the Inari shrine. After she had finished her prayer, she knelt in silence, feeling the peacefulness of nature and earth's beauty entering her.

"Divine force in all things..." Aisawa-san's words came

back to her. Seal removed one of the oranges from her bag. Carefully, she placed it there as an offering.

Sitting down on the soft, shady ground, she began removing her *taus* from its wrapping. *I can also offer some music.* Without calculation or forced effort, but with feeling and love, she began to play. The sounds that poured forth were beautiful and warm, alive and masterful. Her eyes closed, and she felt the dialogue of the Universe flowing from her bow and paw. The song continued for some time—it wasn't a melody she'd ever known—then slowly, sweetly it came to an end. Her eyes opened wide in amazement at what had just happened.

"Thank you!" she whispered to that Divine force, then kissed her *taus* before setting it gently aside. She bowed her forehead to the earth in gratitude.

Wrapping up her *taus* and gathering the sacks, she began walking back to the monastery with a new sensation in her heart. *I want to focus on this moment instead of worrying about the future,* she thought with determination.

CHAPTER 10

THE CEMETERY OF OKUNOIN

WHEN SEAL RETURNED, ENSHO TOLD HER THAT A LARGE family who regularly sponsored the works of the temple were to arrive the next morning. The rest of the day passed quickly as Seal helped with scrubbing floors and arranging rooms in preparation for the visitors.

In the late afternoon, she went to sit beside the pond in the garden. A slight breeze wafted through the burgundy maple leaves as she watched frogs peering out of the water. Around a clump of orange tiger lilies, large black butterflies were feeding.

The sensation of a paw on her shoulder startled her. Looking up, she saw Ensho gazing at her with soft eyes and a loving smile.

"It's time, Seal. We just received an express package from Mukti. It included this map for you. He also instructs that you approach from the west."

Seal looked at the map and scowled. It was notated entirely with Japanese characters. *Surely Mukti knows I can't read Japanese!* She sighed in annoyance. Tucking the map safely into the belt of her robe, she wondered if it would be a help or hindrance.

Slowly and with resignation, she went to her room to collect her belongings one last time, then returned to the front hall, where the monks were gathered.

Gyoki stepped forward and held out a small parcel of salty, fried vegetable sticks. Ensho smiled, concern and compassion mixing on his face.

She looked with fondness at her new friends, then departed in silence.

The sun was still two hours from setting when she reached Okunoin. Standing at the edge of the cemetery, she paused and noticed that even just a few meters ahead, the beautiful green of Koyasan had transformed into a deep, murky darkness. It felt like a bad omen. Bracing herself, she stepped forward.

Seal was immediately reminded that this was a graveyard. Markers and stone statues sprouted up on each side of the path. Some monuments were even placed inside the cave-like bottoms of hollow trees. Small Jizo statues with smooth faces and robed bodies stood scattered throughout the forest. People had placed offerings of red cloth bibs and knitted caps on many of them. Shadowy orbs seemed to be hovering around in the gloom.

She hurried on, not wanting to know what was lurking out of view.

Seal continued deeper and deeper into the forested cemetery. She was trying to follow Mukti's map, but soon it didn't match what she was seeing at all. *There*

should be a road turning off to the left ahead, but instead, it's a straight path, she observed in frustration.

As she stopped to get her bearings, the fluttering orbs she had noticed earlier immediately began descending upon her. Looking up in horror, she realized they were mosquitoes as big as the oranges in her sack. She struggled to swat at them, but they were many and fierce. If she paused for even a second, they settled on her and began feasting. Their needlelike mouths pierced her skin, causing immediate pain and itchiness. Giving up trying to beat them off, she began running again. The insects, which were slow, fell behind.

Eventually, she was forced to pause. *I have to try to look at the map.* Yet again, as soon as she had stopped moving, the mosquitoes quickly plunged into her. Seal shuddered as one came in front of her face, blocking her view of the map. It stared at her with hungry eyes, then began pushing its long mouth through her fur to begin guzzling her blood. Uncomfortable lumps were forming all over her body, making her want to scream. Swatting at the mosquitoes seemed to do nothing. Shoving the map into her belt, she quickly hurried on.

The forest had grown dim. Seal's nose sniffed, sensing change in the air. *Rain is coming.* Picking up her pace, she continued along the narrow trail. Parts of the way were obscured by overgrown vegetation. Following its snaking curves, she made her way deeper and deeper into the cemetery. Suddenly, a wider pathway, strewn with golden leaves, opened to her right.

"Maybe this is it!" she cried hopefully.

Starting down the new path, she squinted and ducked her head, flattening her ears as large raindrops began to fall. The storm intensified as she hurried on. The leaves on the ground were moving and turning. *It's from the rain*, she thought.

On and on she went, as quickly as she could. The larger pathway was easy to follow. *It has to be heading toward a major landmark that will be on the map. Then I'll know where I am.* She doubled her pace as the rain continued soaking her fur.

"Aagh!" A sharp pain brought her suddenly to a halt. It felt like a terrible bee sting.

Looking down at her left leg, Seal saw a long, slimy black creature had attached to her. Aisawa-san's warning came back to her in a flash. "Hiru, *perhaps…slug?*" *Not slug—leech!* She realized now that the movement of the leaves on the ground had been leeches coming out of dormancy, not innocent movement from raindrops.

With her teeth, she grabbed the hideous creature by the tail. It was already gorging and expanding with her blood. She pulled and pulled, but the leech's mouth was firmly affixed to her skin. All she managed to do was stretch it out, causing herself more pain. Several rubbery yanks later, it finally detached. Blood streamed down her leg, staining her white fur. *No time to clean this now.* She frowned, then resumed running as fast as possible.

Zipping down the path, she kept to the center, where the leaves were sparse. A shudder passed through her as she wondered, *What if more leeches are hidden in my fur where I can't see them?*

Turning left and right, speeding through the nightmarish gloom, she continued until she was confronted by the site of a massive pyramid towering before her. It was a formation of lumpy stones that had been mounded together. Sporadic moss and ferns sprouted from the uncanny structure. It was a junction in the path—she had to choose. Would she go left or right? As she neared, she focused her attention, hoping to feel some intuitive prompting about which way to turn. Concentrating, she felt like a magnet was pulling her heart toward the left. She turned, then sped on again.

Not long after passing the pyramid object, Seal came to a low bridge spanning a small river. Tall prayer sticks, standing like soldiers mounted in a line, poked out of the water. *This looks like the place I walked with Ardaas long ago*, she mused as she crossed.

The last dim rays of gloomy light were fading as she continued around a shady bend. Her side was cramping, and each step felt heavy after running so far through the forested burial grounds.

A temple structure loomed ahead. It radiated with an intense, warm glow.

Approaching cautiously, Seal quietly entered. There was a strong and familiar presence. *Ardaas must be here.* She continued on with a new hopefulness.

Seal padded along, searching for clues. *This temple seems completely empty, but I feel like I'm not alone.*

Rounding a corner, her nose crinkled up tightly as the intense smell of gorilla overwhelmed her. There was nothing in the room except one small, iridescent emerald feather, delicately arched on the stone floor. Surveying the room, she searched the shadows beyond the reach of the lanterns. For one moment, a terrible face, the same one Aisawa-san had painted, seemed to leer from the darkness. She blinked, and it was gone.

Just as she began retracing her steps, an uncanny, guttural roar ripped through the temple, echoing off the stone. Seal turned to see the full form of Kadir propelling toward her. He moved with unbelievable speed and agility. His arms swung forward, the weight of his massive body shaking the earth as he barreled straight for her. Anger filled his rolling eyes. His scarred face and yellow teeth were twisted into a ferocious snarl.

"You will never be together, *never*!" the ape shouted. Galloping forward, he used his huge, flat palm hit Seal with tremendous force as he passed over her. The power of the strike lifted her body into the air, and she thudded to the ground, unconscious.

CHAPTER 11

ALL IS LOST

Seal's eyelids fluttered slightly. There was light. Not the orange glow of the lanterns, but a white light. She opened her eyes fully. *I must have been here all night.*

She lay there a few moments, remembering Kadir's words and the terror she had felt while seeing him charge toward her.

Slowly sitting up, she looked around fearfully. *Is he still here? No, I'm alone now.* She sighed with both relief and frustration at having her encounter with him end without even knowing if Ardaas had been there, let alone saving him.

The sky was filled with a silvery glow that warned of more rain. A cold breeze was blowing through the temple and over her aching body. The sound of monks could be heard in the far distance, performing their duties.

Ahead of her, the solitary feather still lay on the ground. The green plume seemed to emit a radiance of its own. Crawling over, she picked it up, then slid it carefully into her embroidered pouch.

It was clear that Kadir had gone. Seal had missed her chance.

Her head was pounding, and her body felt stiff with pain. A depression was overcoming her. *I really don't know what to do now.* Slowly standing on trembling legs, she began making her way out of the temple. *I feel like I've been slammed into a cement wall,* she thought as she struggled forward.

As she neared the bridge, a familiar tiny brown shape became visible. Her heart warmed in a way it never had before.

"Mukti!" she called out with joy. There he was, his little beard looking as much like a piece of wool stuck to his face as ever. From the way its edges drew up, she could tell he was smiling. He had been studying a set of accordion-folded maps.

"Hello, Seal!" he sang out before continuing in a serious tone. "You lost the trail. Kadir was seen far from here this morning. We must hurry."

Seal began to remove the crusted blood from her leg. It was the first chance she'd had to take care of it.

"What happened?" Mukti asked, watching her with concern.

"Hiru." Seal shuddered, recalling the horrible leech.

Mukti gasped, his little eyes shifting back and forth, surveying the ground. "Keep to the center of the path," he instructed.

"And out of the leaves!" Seal added knowingly as they began their journey.

Cicadas droned loudly in all directions as the two companions retraced the route out of the gloomy cemetery.

Seal had no energy left for speed, so the mosquitoes were once again hovering around her. She began swatting at them, though she knew it was no use. "Why aren't they bothering you, Mukti?"

"I soaked my beard in camphor oil," he replied with confidence.

Seal had a crafty idea. "Hey, Mukti, want to ride on my back?"

He eyed her suspiciously.

"Those leeches down there are almost as big as you!"

A frightened look came onto his face, and he hurriedly hopped up and sat behind her neck.

Seal smiled. *Camphor for two.*

They eventually made their way back to the monastery. It didn't take nearly as long to return with Mukti's expert guidance.

As they entered the foyer, Ensho appeared. "Seal, come to my chamber," he said in a serious tone.

She followed him somberly down the hall. *Maybe he's angry with me for failing.*

After they were seated on the round, black floor cushions in the fox's room, he began to speak. "You look troubled. What is it?" he softly prompted her.

With a long face, Seal stared down at the grass matting. There was something that had bothered her all along about this venture. After some moments, she looked up and asked, "How will I find Ardaas, or know if I have found him, if I don't even know what he looks like?"

The fox's amber eyes fixed on her as he listened. Then he closed them tightly in contemplation before replying, "Ardaas needs no image to be found. You will feel him. Trust this. Move to that place where the action becomes stillness, and you will see all clearly."

Seal felt confused by his mysterious reply. Where action becomes stillness? That didn't seem to make any sense. And how would that allow her to see?

Just then, a bell sounded. The soulful fox touched the crown of her head with compassion and blessing, then stood up and bowed to her. Seal stood and returned the bow. She was still confused but also felt her heart brimming with humility and gratitude. *No one is upset with me, even though I failed. They still have faith in me,* she realized with surprise and relief.

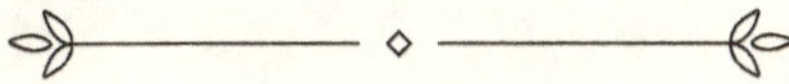

It was time to leave the monastery. Mukti had the route planned out.

Ensho came forward and gave Seal a long coil of rope, made the *shimenawa* way. "You may need this before your mission is completed."

Seal accepted the gift and hugged the cat-eyed fox tenderly.

Gyoki spoke up next in his gruff voice. "Remember to use ancient sleeping technique." He smiled and bowed.

Seal smiled and nodded, then bowed.

Mukti and Seal set off down the mountain road, then boarded the cable car and descended to the bottom, where the train awaited. Mukti left to speak with the trainmaster in hushed tones.

"Transport has been arranged on the Express-Express," he said when he returned. "This is the fastest way—forty-five minutes to Kyoto."

Seal sighed. *Sure, why not?*

They boarded the train—which, through Mukti's persuasion, had somehow become the Express-Express—and sped off toward their next destination.

CHAPTER 12

THE CORMORANTS OF KYOTO

THE TRAIN PULLED INTO THE BUSY KYOTO STATION.

Seal wasn't too surprised when Mukti turned to her on the platform and announced, "I must leave you. I have some urgent work to complete for Tansen." She couldn't help but wish her dear, old teacher didn't need Mukti's assistance quite so much. "A local guide should arrive shortly," the mouse continued. "Good luck!" With that, he smiled, turned, and disappeared through the crowd.

Seal remained on the busy platform, feeling like she was in the center of a colony of industrious ants. No guide was visible, and she felt helpless.

Her gaze drifted to a spot in the distance, where a patch of bare floor was saturated by a pool of sunshine. *A nap sounds heavenly. Surely five minutes won't hurt?* She began to make her way toward the sunny beacon.

"Coming, Seal?" a croaky voice called out from behind her. Turning, she saw the elegant, sleek form of an inky-black cormorant staring at her. "I am your guide in Kyoto," the bird continued. "Please come quickly. First lunch, then important work."

"Who are you?" Seal asked as she hurried to keep up with the bird's strange walk.

"Zochi," the cormorant answered. His wings fluttered open, and the dark feathers flashed with a shiny blueish glow. It reminded Seal of flowing water. He craned his neck up to its full length. Zochi's mustard-colored bill clacked, and his bright turquoise eyes surveyed the scene. Then, lowering his head, he began pushing his way through the crowd like a little bulldozer.

Seal followed closely behind, and they soon emerged from the station.

As they rushed by, Seal caught glimpses of interesting shrines, strangely shaped trees, and curiosity shops.

They stopped outside a small restaurant. It had a window displaying lifelike sculptures of the various foods served inside. Seal's stomach rumbled like thunder. It smelled so good.

They entered and sat in a cozy booth. Zochi ordered two bowls of ramen, which quickly arrived in gigantic bowls. Seal licked her muzzle and grabbed her chopsticks. Swimming in a huge sea of savory broth were crinkly noodles, slices of the white-and-pink spiral thing she had eaten at Aisawa-san's, half of a hardboiled egg, bean sprouts, and to the side there were some flat, crunchy seaweed squares. It was a veritable feast!

Seal slurped up the long noodles as she watched Zochi grab morsels in his bill, then raise his head to the

heavens, opening wide to chug the pieces down. She stifled a giggle, then continued slurping and munching.

Lifting their bowls, they drank the dregs of the broth. Then, with rounded bellies, they both slouched back in their seats.

Zochi's bright eyes fixed on Seal, then he spoke. "Kadir was spotted in Kyoto last night. We know where he's stationed." He paused as the waitress brought them what looked like two round buns, then immediately pecked into his.

Seal poked a paw at hers, then took a small bite. It was filled with red beans, but they were as sweet as candy. Chomping off big mouthfuls, she savored the unusual treat.

"We'll discuss more later," Zochi announced. "Now we'll go rest. Soon it will be time for work."

They made their way to a local river where Zochi labored with several other cormorants. He waddled over to a shady tree, where a sort of camp was set up, and huddled down for sleep. Seal chose an open spot on the soft grass and contentedly curled up, feeling the sun's healing rays baking her little body.

Some hours later, she awoke as the coolness of twilight descended.

The cormorants were already awake and working at preparing a boat. A large metal basket, which had been filled with wood, was suspended over the edge. Zochi was busy setting it on fire. "The flames will guide us and entice fish," he explained.

As dusk fell, they cast off. The birds stood tall as they guided the craft downriver. The work began in earnest as they took turns diving into the dark water and returning with fish in their bills. Seal helped by placing caught fish in baskets and, now and then, throwing more fuel onto the fire.

After several hours, they returned to the shoreside camp. Everyone collapsed, exhausted from the night's work. The cormorants were sleek and clean from their constant diving, while Seal was greasy and covered in soot from the smoky fire. She also smelled very fishy, but she didn't mind that.

Taking small steps, she waded in at the river's edge. It was so cold! She shivered as she went in farther, letting the river's current wash the filth away. Refreshed, she returned to the cormorants on the shore.

It was that curious time of day when the dawn's light was beginning to reenter the sky. The subtle glow made you ask yourself if it was really the sun rising or just a mirage. The sky continued to brighten with a purple-blue glow.

Seal felt inspired and unwrapped her *taus*. Softly, she began to play.

The cormorants raised their heads in a swoon, entranced by the power of the music.

Seal's bow eventually stopped, the last vibrations fading from the strings, then silence…

After a restful pause, the cormorants fluttered back to life and discussions began.

"Kadir is in a rage about being found and tracked," Zochi said. "He injured several locals who happened to cross his path. He's stationed in Kyoto's most unique fortification, Nijo Castle."

"A castle?" Seal asked, concerned. She only knew of fairy-tale castles with high stone walls.

"Yes, a castle," Zochi continued. "It's a massive wooden complex made hundreds of years ago with the highest craftsmanship. It has nightingale floors. They are made to squeak and chirp under the most delicate footstep. No one can enter or exit unnoticed."

Seal took this in, then said, "Well how can I…soto technique!"

Zochi's bill dropped open in surprise. "Soto? You know the art of secret walking?" He let out a cackle and smiled. "Truly, that's just the thing."

The other cormorants looked at their cat companion with awe.

Zochi took a long, thin stick in his bill and began scratching a map in the muddy soil. "A moat encircles the castle. The front gate is the only place to approach." He marked another spot with an X. "You must scale the wall here. Inside, you will encounter the nightingale floors. They are made with a system of pegs and nails that make the whole floor sound like a flock of birds. If anyone lays a toe on them, the whole castle is alerted.

Your soto technique must not fail." He emphasized his words by tapping the map with his stick.

They sat in silence for a moment.

Seal doubted her ability to succeed. She was still very new at the soto technique and hadn't had a chance to practice much since leaving Mi-chan.

"Ardaas is most likely being hidden in the central chamber, here." Zochi pointed. "You must pass through the long halls and two large rooms. But"—he tilted his head—"how will we get you over the gate?"

"Would this help?" Seal removed the *shimenawa* rope Ensho had given her from her travel bag.

"Magnificent!" Zochi exclaimed. He admired the rope. "A strong, supple yet delicate piece of work. We must get you into the castle tonight. There's no moon, so it will be our best chance. But first, we must do something about this." He poked his stick at Seal's long white fur. "This cannot be seen."

The cormorants scattered to search for supplies, then returned. Seal looked on, worried, as they dropped an old black rubber diving suit and a tin of charcoal dust in front of her.

"It will have to do," Zochi replied in positive tones but with a doubtful look.

The cormorants helped pull the rubber suit over her fur.

"Ow! Careful, it pinches," she cried.

They continued by covering the white parts of her face with a thick layer of charcoal dust, which made her sneeze. The birds stood back, surveying the results.

"The tail is gray—it doesn't show," one cormorant

remarked. The group suddenly erupted in laughter at the strange sight before them.

Zochi, who had remained silent, cleared his throat. "What about the foot?"

The group fell into immediate silence as all eyes were drawn to Seal's one white back paw. It was extremely eye-catching.

Zochi appeared to think for a moment, then disappeared into a storage shed and returned with one small black sock drooping from his bill. "Not sophisticated, but sufficient," he said as he pulled the sock over the offending foot. "She still looks like a cat…" Pacing back and forth, he looked at Seal while considering the situation. Finally, he stepped forward and strapped Seal's cloth-wrapped *taus* to her back. "Wow! That creates a fantastic silhouette. You look more like a hunchbacked monster now."

Seal felt overwhelming humiliation and doom.

Zochi picked up his stick and tapped at the map

he'd drawn in the mud again. "Memorize this. Castle, garden wall, palace walls, central chamber—reached from either end by these rooms and halls. Remember, the halls and some of the chambers have nightingale floors. Got it? Keep to the shadows. Skirt the wall until it runs close to the palace. You should be able to blend into other objects for cover."

Seal stared at the map, trying to take everything in and mentally prepare for the task ahead of her. She couldn't shake the fear that this wouldn't end well.

CHAPTER 13

ARDAAS

NIGHT CAME, AND ZOCHI, SEAL, AND THE OTHER COR-morants mounted a bicycle rickshaw and rode toward Nijo Castle. Pulling over when they were near, they got off in the shade of a large cypress tree. Everything was dark and still. The odd companions crept silently toward the castle gate.

Seal tied a knot at one end of her rope. Grabbing it in his beak, Zochi flew high over the wall, dropping it where it would catch on the knobby wood of the massive carved gate posts.

Seal tugged at her end and felt it bite successfully into the structure. She pulled again with all her might to make sure it was secure. Then, taking a deep breath, she steadied herself and began climbing. It was slow going, and her sock-covered back foot kept slipping.

At the top of the gate, she used the friction of the rubber suit to move like a caterpillar. Under the cover of an overhanging roof edge, she paused to pull the rope up, then dropped it to the opposite side. Shimmying down, she descended to the castle grounds.

Slinking along in the deepest shadows and creeping low to the earth, she moved from the gate to the castle wall. All was eerily silent and empty.

Seal rounded a corner, then froze. The scent of gorilla was strong. Kadir must have been in the gardens just moments ago. Looking down, she gulped, realizing the depressed earth she was standing in was the gorilla's footprint. *My whole body fits inside it!*

Diving under a shrub, she quietly removed the rubber suit and sock, but felt some intuition telling her to strap her *taus* back on.

Sneaking forward through the night, she made her way to one of the paper doors and began cutting an entrance with her claws. She had barely placed one paw inside when she was met with a loud chirrup, which echoed through the dimly lit hall. Seal froze. *No! The nightingale floors run all the way to the edge. No room to prepare my stance*, she thought. She remained frozen, waiting to see if anyone was coming.

Looking around, she calculated the best moves to start with. Carefully balancing, she leaped on pointed paws, navigating the first hallway. There was a thin ledge along the wall at the farthest side of the room, and she headed straight for it. Reaching it, she grabbed on, balancing her weight and catching her breath.

It all looks so different from Zochi's map, she thought, then realized the walls were movable, like at Koyasan. The rooms took on different formations as they were slid open or closed.

Preparing to advance, she calculated her next landing point and began. Turn, touch—glide. *Swoosh—chirp!* The floor sounded out immediately under her poorly placed paw. Abruptly, Seal stopped. *My technique needs improvement*, she anxiously thought before moving forward.

An angry warning call sounded from one of the nearby chambers. Seal held her breath as she heard the sounds of a heavy creature charging. Ten meters away, a gigantic gorilla appeared in the doorway of an adjacent room. Swiftly and with great power, the dark, hairy mass swung forward in gallops across the floor. The ancient wooden building trembled under its weight.

Seal shuddered. *Is it Kadir?* Flattening herself toward the ground, she held her breath, watching from the shadows.

The ape's flattened head turned slowly as he scanned the room. His nostrils flared with each powerful breath, and his eyes appeared to have a reddish glow. After several moments of stillness, the ape turned with disappointment and departed. By chance, he hadn't seen her in the gloom.

Seal's heart was pounding as she remained motionless. The sounds of several angry gorillas vocalizing in the distance flooded through the castle. *That brute was just a guard, then. One of many, it seems,* she realized in horror.

Moving with caution, she continued along the wall. A small painted panel started to give way under her weight. *Another door!* Sliding it aside, she crept into a low, dark passage. It was too small for any gorilla to navigate. Testing the wood with one paw, Seal heard a soft chirp. *More nightingale floors.* She sighed, preparing her stance, then began soto technique again.

She navigated through the limited space and traversed the final length of narrow passage using a series of acrobatic maneuvers.

At the end of the low hall, she popped out through a hidden doorway at the far end and found herself directly in the central chamber. Bright lanterns lit the large room, revealing ornate decorations. The ceiling was painted with golden geometrical shapes. The gilded walls shimmered with decorations of cedar and pine trees. But the room was empty. It was obvious that Ardaas was not there. Raising her nose, Seal sniffed the air to gather information. The gorilla's strong smell was lingering. *They must have been in here recently.* Narrowing her eyes, she navigated forward.

The only option ahead was a large doorway on the opposite wall. The floor in the central chamber was made of silent tatami grass matting. *I can finally move freely.* She sighed in relief.

Skirting the perimeter of the room in a low, stealthy prowl, Seal paused now and then, making sure no gorillas were coming. Then she slipped noiselessly through the wide, open panel.

This area of the castle was very dark and musty. Seal crept several paces into the shadowy room when she was startled by the sounds of another guard approaching. Quickly, she slid herself next to a cabinet, peering out as he hurried past. The smell of the apes was getting more intense. *Soon there might not be a place to hide from them,* she realized fearfully.

Her eyes began to water and her nose crinkled tightly as she moved forward once again. The dusky chamber ended, and a brightly lit room lay beyond. She inched toward the doorway.

It was a midsized room, even more amazing than the last decorative chamber. Beautiful large green trees, hawks, and fierce tigers embellished the brilliant walls. The ceiling squares were adorned in sky-blue and green flowers. There were no gorillas in the room, but it smelled strongly of them.

There was a strange buzzing noise periodically coming from a small object at the far end of the chamber. Inching cautiously forward, Seal went to inspect it.

A little box made of woven reeds with a pointed top sat in the center of a low table. *It's a tiny house,* she realized in amazement. Her head tipped sideways as the enclosure began vibrating and rocking slightly. Small windows laced with thin metal bars covered two sides of the house. *What's making it move?* Curiously, she leaned in closer. The buzzing began again, and a stream of air blew into her eyes. Squinting, she could only make out ripples of shadow and light.

The miniature house became still, and Seal could see an emerald-and-ruby hummingbird inside. Its breath was labored. *It's not a house*, she realized. *It's a prison.*

Seal's instincts were triggered by the close proximity to her natural prey. Her first impulse was to lunge and attack the little bird. Drawing back a paw, she prepared to knock the prison to the floor and devour its contents. But then the hummingbird's long beak poked out through one of the barred windows. It looked at her with tiny, steady eyes, and spoke.

"Seal!" the bird whispered in amazement. "You found me!"

For a moment, she was paralyzed, then fearfully she inched her face close to the barred window. "Ardaas?" Her voice came shakily.

Could it possibly be? It certainly didn't look like the Ardaas she remembered. Closing her eyes, she recalled Tansen's words, *"Remember his soul, not his shell."*

Seal focused her attention, becoming aware of her breath. Placing her paws on the wicker prison, she closed her eyes and concentrated on feeling the energy of life within. In the darkness of her mind, a symbol suddenly appeared in gold.

What did it mean? A warmth rose up from the depths of her body. She was filled with a powerful feeling of peace and love. The symbol faded away into darkness, and a memory vision began to play in her mind.

She was in a strange land. Leaves rustled on a fresh wind, which smelled strongly of flowers. Warm sun was beating down. Ardaas was next to her in his cat body. They were both wearing some sort of cloth wrapped around their heads. Standing beneath a large, low-hanging tree, they were watching a host of hummingbirds buzzing around nectar-filled blossoms.

They looked up in amazement at the spectacle. Turning to Ardaas, Seal was surprised to see a great white light pulsing in his heart center. It was so intense she could barely look at it.

She peered back up at the swarming hummingbirds and saw that each one also had a strong, pulsating brilliance in its heart center. Swirling, diving, circling the tree like tiny subatomic particles. Each one moving with the energy of the Divine, each one emanating love and union.

Looking down now at her own heart, she saw the gleaming pulse was there too. Then the vision faded, and darkness returned to her closed eyes.

"Ardaas… Divine force in everything…" she whispered. "Trees, rocks, water…hummingbirds. Ardaas, it is you. I recognize your soul!" Seal opened her eyes. She could see a faint white glow pulsing within the small basket prison.

Just then, a door in the back of the room forcefully slid open. There stood the unmistakable, furious form of Kadir. A guttural inhale followed by a powerful, nerve-shattering roar tore through the room. His huge mouth gaped, showing yellow, chipped teeth. The ape flung his head from side to side in a quick, jerky fashion. Standing to full height, he pounded his chest, a haunting sound. Swinging forward, he lunged from the doorway to the table in one swift motion, grabbing the wicker prison with such horrifying force it seemed it might be crushed. Turning around, he then propelled himself back out the door while letting out a terrifying war cry.

Seal was petrified. A dark, shadowy cloud had seemed to surround Kadir's body. Her mind was seared with the twisted, murderous look on his face. Then, from far regions of the castle, she heard the sounds of charging apes moving toward the chamber. The wooden structure shook as if from an earthquake under their weight, and the chirping of the floor became deafening. Danger was approaching fast.

Divine force in everything? What do I do? she asked herself. Her mind shut down, and her body began moving automatically. Eyes wide with terror, she noticed her paw reaching behind her, loosening the *taus*. What? Now? How could this be a good idea? *Shouldn't I at least try to run or hide?*

But she didn't hide. She found herself sitting right there in the open center of the chamber. Something beyond her own will was functioning through her now as her *taus* and bow came into position before her. She began to play, and the sound was different from anything she had heard before. It felt as if a musical voice was speaking with intoxicating strength through the instrument, and her arm was being guided by unseen hands.

The apes reached the doorway, and one by one, the resonant *taus* stopped them in their tracks. All sense of urgency drained from their faces, and their eyes clouded over as though they were in a dream. Collapsing to the floor, completely entranced, they remained in a swoon. The music intensified, picking up speed. It pulsed like rhythmic heartbeats.

As Seal kept playing, she took small steps toward the door where the apes lay. She scooted around the motionless group, the music surrounding them in a blanket of hypnotic sound. Moving farther and farther into the dark corridor, she slowly faded her song to an end and began to run.

The gorillas confusedly began to regain their senses. Soon their yells of outrage made soto technique unnecessary. Seal beat a quick retreat, running all the way to the castle gardens.

Outside, the gate sagged with a huge, gaping hole. Kadir was gone. Seal wondered if Ardaas was still alive or if he'd been crushed completely in the gorilla's fury.

She sprinted across the open expanse toward the hole. As she neared it, Kadir suddenly swung into view, blocking her escape. His hairy fist snatched at her, but he only grasped the *taus* on her back. It ripped off and was crushed into thousands of useless splinters of wood and string. Seal ran on.

The rickshaw was gone. In a way, it didn't matter—

it wouldn't have been able to travel fast enough for her to make an escape.

In full sprint, she turned and began zigzagging through the streets of Kyoto, farther and farther away from the castle. But she was new to this city and had no sense of direction. There was no way for her to return to the cormorants' home.

After several kilometers, she slackened her pace but kept moving. Her only instinct was to get as far from Kadir's lair as possible. She navigated toward the mountains on the opposite side of the city. After about an hour, she finally stopped and collapsed at the base of a massive tree. Surrendering to exhaustion, she fell into a deep sleep.

CHAPTER 14

THE SILVER TANUKI

SEAL AWOKE EARLY, GAZING UPWARD THROUGH MASSIVE, twisted branches overhead. She was resting in a nook created by large moss-covered roots. An ancient camphor tree towered above her with its tiny leaves and fantastic curving limbs. Looking sidelong at the trunk, she realized it was thick enough to be at least eight hundred years old. She felt like she was resting in the lap of a great-grandmother.

Her head hurt, and she felt nauseated. Sitting up slowly, she looked around. The tree was growing on a small hillside. Above and behind it rose a simple single-level structure with the characteristic look of a traditional Japanese temple.

Trying to shake the sleep from her aching body, Seal made her way up the hillside and peered in through the door, which had been left open. The room inside had no furniture, and grass matting covered the floor. The wall panels were white with large red and gold flowers on the bottom portions. On each side of the space, just below ceiling level, hung a row of pictures show-ing people in colorful robes.

The doors of the room were open, revealing other parts of the temple. The building's outer panels were also open, giving access to the grounds behind it. Seal slowly padded over to look out. It was an ornamental garden, similar to the one at Koyasan but ten times as big. There was a huge pond, many different decorative trees, rocks, and a stone bridge. The far side was bor-dered by a forest of large evergreens.

Seal sat down on a wooden walkway that looked out over the water. Her head was throbbing, and her stomach was cramping and gurgling in an unpleasant way. *Soon, I'm going to need a toilet for more than one reason,* she thought with anxiety. Slumping over, she stared at the ground, breathing slowly.

Memories from the night before flooded her mind. There was a feeling of amazement at having found Ardaas. His bird body had certainly been a surprise. Yet she had recognized some deeper part of her friend. *It was like reuniting with a loved one, not like meeting someone for the first time. How strange, beautiful, and unexpected,* she reflected.

But now what? Even if Kadir remained in the castle, there was little chance of regaining entry. What had happened to the cormorants? Had they fled to safety? Or had they also fallen victim to Kadir? She wasn't even sure of where she was, let alone what to do next.

She felt very hot and was sweating profusely. The painful throbbing in her head, the cramps, and the nausea were getting worse. She vomited then collapsed onto her side. Blinking slowly, she watched as everything turned fuzzy. The fur around her mouth was scraggly, damp, and sour.

Thunk, thunk, thunk, thunk... The sound of footsteps drew near.

Seal lifted her head with effort and saw the form of an old silver tanuki in Buddhist robes, standing over her. He spoke softly. It sounded like a question, but it was in Japanese. She couldn't understand one word.

The strength ebbed out of her, and her head flopped down in pain, unable to move.

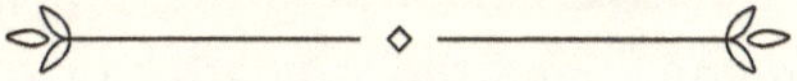

Seal began to experience convulsing shivers followed by intolerable heat. Her body was drenched in sweat, so when the chills returned, it didn't matter how many blankets she was under; it still felt like she was in a pile of cold snow. A pain was radiating from her spine that felt unbearable. Sometimes she woke up just enough to vomit. Throughout everything, she kept experiencing the pounding pain in her head and body. The slightest movements were excruciating. Rarely, her eyes would open to dim light, and she might see the silver tanuki gazing down at her compassionately or wiping the perspiration from her brow with a soft cloth. She had no sense of time. It could have been one long, awful night, or a month. Seal was completely insensible. Strange dreams haunted her, with visions of Kadir, spiders, and orbs that turned from throbbing dark shadows to shimmering green.

Eventually, she woke up fully, and everything seemed clear again. She lay there, staring at the room. It was early evening. Was it the same day she had collapsed? There was no way to know. She tried to sit up but was so weak she could barely move. Looking down at her body, she saw she had become very thin and scraggly. Her fur didn't even look long anymore and had become patchy in places. It was shocking. Quite some time must have passed, then.

Glancing toward the open door of the room, she could see the pond and walkway beyond. A robed form was sitting facing the water in meditation. A vague memory of the silver tanuki returned to her. Perhaps it was him? She mustered the strength to rise and feebly, with shaking legs, made her way from the floor futon she had been sleeping on toward the robed figure.

Yes, it was the aged tanuki. He was in very deep meditation and didn't seem to realize he had company.

Seal sat down next to him, as straight as her weakness would allow, and brought her breath into a deep, slow rhythm. The meditation felt like soothing medicine to her exhausted system. The sound of the water, a soft breeze, the buzzing of dragonflies... Many things entered her awareness, but she let them fade into the background and maintained her focus.

After some time, Seal felt a gentle paw on her head and opened her eyes. The silver tanuki looked down at her, his eyes moist with tears. She could tell he was relieved at her recovery. They sat in silence awhile longer, gazing out on the pond as dusk fell, then he carried her back into her room.

Over the next several days, she began to recover. She was now able to eat, which helped her gain strength. After about a week, she was able to help the tanuki with small chores. They meditated together, and she rested deeply at night.

Before she knew it, three more weeks had passed, and her health had returned in full. Seal now worked hard alongside the old tanuki daily with gardening, cooking, and cleaning jobs. The labor gave her exercise, and the nutritious meals they shared continued to rebuild her strength.

But she was troubled. Her mind constantly churned over the situation that needed solving. *How will I find Kadir and Ardaas or the cormorants?* She didn't know where she was or how long she had been there—the tanuki only spoke Japanese, and she only spoke English.

Then one morning after breakfast, she came upon her caregiver while he was writing letters. An idea inspired her, and she motioned to him that she would like to use some paper and the ink brush. She drew the river and a boat with a burning basket, then the cormorants. Next to them, she drew herself, then tore that piece off. The tanuki watched her with puzzlement. She made sure he was looking, then held up the little Seal drawing and moved it to be with the cormorants again. She repeated the action several times, pulling the picture of herself away and replacing it. Would he understand?

A slow smile spread across his face. Taking up the little Seal drawing, he moved it to the fishing birds and set it down. Then he slowly walked to the next room,

where a large wooden cabinet stood in the corner. He pulled out a travel bag, bamboo sunshades, thin brown cloaks, and a long walking staff. He had understood!

Seal was elated and sorry at the same time. *I hate to leave this peaceful place. But my heart wants desperately to find Ardaas as soon as possible.*

The old tanuki handed Seal a small bag with a water canteen and some snacks. He threw a small travel cloak over her and placed a sunshade on her head. Then they set out.

After about an hour, they reached the river. The tanuki gestured and spoke. It seemed he was trying to ask if she knew which direction they should go—left or right.

Seal surveyed both directions as far as she could. Nothing looked familiar. Closing her eyes, she concentrated on her heart, asking, *Where have I been before?* A strong feeling, which could only be called intuition, told her south. She pointed her outstretched paw, and the two set off following the riverbank.

A couple hours had passed when they came upon a scene that looked very familiar, but she didn't see any cormorants. There were, however, telltale signs that they had been there—scars from a fishing boat being pulled up on the bank for repair, remnants from the fires, and debris from the fish.

Seal gazed down in uncertainty, then up at her wise companion. She had no idea what to do next and looked into his dark eyes pleadingly.

Her guide sat down, gesturing for Seal to do the same, then he began to meditate.

She fidgeted anxiously, letting out a heavy sigh as her face fell in frustration. *I feel so far from finding Ardaas.*

The old tanuki's silence grew heavier. Seal began to notice a low hum in the air. Mystified, she looked around, trying to discover the source of the sound. *It's getting louder,* she thought with alarm. Soon it was like the crashing of an ocean. Placing her paws over her ears, she looked over at the tanuki. He didn't seem to notice anything unusual. He simply remained in the stillness of his meditation.

After a while, he abruptly stood up and quickly moved forward in a trancelike state. Seal followed along, jogging so she wouldn't fall behind.

After some time, they reached a thick grove of trees near the bank. Without a word or gesture, the tanuki went into the grove and lay flat on the ground. Seal stared at him for a few moments, then lay down as well, once she realized he wasn't going to budge. His eyes closed tightly, and he seemed to be back in the stillness of meditation.

Relieved to be off her feet, Seal spread her thin cloak over herself. It was getting dark. She rested deeply as the warm wind carrying scents from the river wafted over them.

As dawn approached, a boat pulled up to the shore near the grove. The last coals of a fire were smoldering in a basket hanging from one end. A crew of shadows waddled onto the shore. Their movements looked weary.

Seal's eyes popped open. Joyfully, she beheld

Zochi's face peering down at her with a look of stunned curiosity in his bright turquoise eyes.

"Where in the world have you been, Seal?" he crooned. "We've been looking for you for weeks!" With a sigh of contentment, he nuzzled his beak into her fur.

CHAPTER 15

IK ONKAR

SEAL SAT UP. THE SILVER TANUKI WAS CROUCHING DOWN by the riverside, filling his canteen. He stood, smiled at her, then waved farewell. She watched as he began retracing the path they had traveled the day before. *I can't let him go without a proper goodbye,* she thought with urgency.

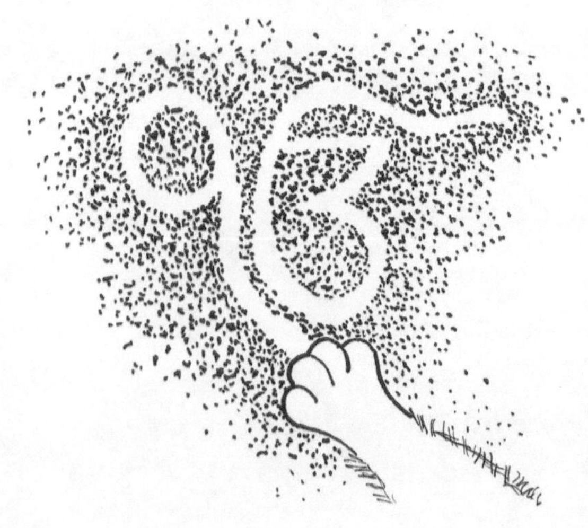

Running to him, she grabbed on to his loose sleeve. The tanuki turned, and Seal reached her paws as far as she could around him, giving him a huge hug. Her eyes narrowed as she breathed in his earthy scent and felt his warm arms embracing her. Looking up, she saw he had tears in his eyes. He patted her lovingly on the head, then they parted. Seal was sorry to see him go. She would never be able to repay him for his help and kindness.

The cormorants crowded around her, and Seal began relating the details of the events since the failed rescue attempt at Nijo Castle. A solemn silence fell over them as she finished talking.

"We heard Kadir break through the gate," Zochi said. "Then we were forced to drive off because some guard apes started coming toward us. By the time you came out, we must have been on the opposite side of the castle. It was too dangerous to go back. There was no way to find you safely and escape together..." Zochi's head hung down sadly, and his words trailed off.

Seal patted his back to comfort him. "We all did the best we could that night, even if we weren't successful."

"Well, why don't we get some food?" Zochi suggested, clearly trying to ease the situation. "How about Indian?"

"I'm not hungry, but I'll go with you," Seal replied.

They walked through Kyoto, down Sanjo-dori Street until they came to a two-story building, where they climbed the stairs and entered an Indian restaurant. It was a little disorienting, walking from the Japanese surroundings outside into a room decorated with elephants and Hindu gods and goddesses. Upbeat Indian folk music was playing loudly from a sound system overhead.

A young-looking woman, with wavy black hair pulled back into a soft bun and covered with a sheer scarf, guided them to a table.

"Seal, this is Prajna," Zochi informed her. "She is one of our closest friends." He smiled gently.

Seal felt that the woman's large hazel eyes were radiating love, wisdom, and compassion.

Zochi told Prajna about the recent happenings, while the cormorants ordered food and began talking among themselves.

Seal felt depressed. Staring down at the tablecloth, she traced the handle of a spoon with her paw. Ardaas was gone, perhaps dead. Her *taus* had been destroyed. She feared the gorillas—Kadir was not a force to trifle with. Seeing him alongside his guards, she now knew that he towered over them. His sheer physical strength combined with his destructive agenda made her feel so small and helpless. *What will happen when I face him again?* she pondered fearfully.

Prajna had gone to the kitchen and returned with some fried onion appetizers. The cormorants immediately dove into the crispy treats and began devouring them. The peaceful Indian woman stayed a moment, seeming to notice Seal's depressed state.

"Seal," she said in her lovely accent, "will you help me make lunch?"

Sighing, Seal got up and followed her into the kitchen.

Prajna directed her to a board, atop which sat a pile of dough used to make naan and roti bread. "Will you please roll these into small balls and flatten them?" she asked.

Seal trilled in assent. *Helping with food might make life feel almost normal again*, she mused to herself.

She began shaping little spheres from the dough, pressing them down with her paws. Then Prajna took them and patted and clapped them between her hands before cooking them. The work was meditative, and Seal's mind began to quiet. After some time, she became so still, she dropped the dough, and her paw began tracing a pattern into the flour dusting the table. She looked down. It was the golden symbol she had seen in the darkness of her mind earlier.

ੴ

Seal looked at it, trying to understand what it meant.

Prajna glanced over to see why Seal had stopped working. Seeing the pattern in the flour, she smiled. "Do you know this?" she asked.

"No, but I saw it in my mind, and I can't forget it. Do you know what it is?"

With reverence, Prajna whispered, "*Ik Onkar*... Yes, I know it."

"What does '*Ik Onkar*' mean?" Seal asked.

"A simple explanation is that everything in creation and what created it are one and the same."

Seal thought out loud, "One source… Divine force in all things…"

Prajna smiled again, looking at Seal with affection. "Yes, dear, that's another way to put it."

Just then, a little brown shape covered in flour came out from behind the tandoor oven. It was Mukti! He was helping Prajna too. His proximity to the clay oven had given his beard a slightly golden hue around the edges.

"You're here, Mukti?" Seal asked, happy to see him.

"I wouldn't miss Prajna's cooking for the world!" he exclaimed. "Isn't the naan ready to be baked yet?"

Seal hurriedly began patting more dough balls. Prajna left the two friends and finished preparing the rest of the lunch, after which they all went out to rejoin the cormorants.

Mukti munched large mouthfuls of warm, buttery naan as he asked Seal, "What now? It seems like your best chance is lost."

Seal pushed the food around on her plate dejectedly, remaining silent. She didn't have an answer for the mouse, and she couldn't eat, not even this delicious food.

Eventually the others finished their meals and sat in silence, letting their food digest. Prajna, who had gone into the back room, reappeared with some white cloth folded in her arms. "I believe you'll be needing this where you're going next," she said. "Mukti, do you have the maps for Punjab?"

The mouse looked up. "I do!" he exclaimed. "I've been itching for a chance to use them again." His beard flapped as he told them all about Punjab, in India, the land of his ancestors, where legends of gurus, powerful yogis, gods, and goddesses abounded.

Their kind hostess gave him the smallest bundle of cloth. Bowing, he squeaked, "Oh! I've waited a long time for one of these!" She presented the larger cloth to Seal, who was grateful but puzzled.

"You'll know what to do with it when the time comes," Prajna said. "Keep it safe and clean in the meantime." They stowed the fabric carefully in their travel bags, then the graceful woman embraced Seal and kissed her on the forehead. "Keep up your spirits, little one!"

Seal felt her heart center warming with love, and tears welled up in her eyes. She felt like she was experiencing the love of the mother she had never known. "I hate to leave," she cried. "It feels so good and safe with you."

Prajna looked at her compassionately. "Wherever you go, you will find what you expect to find. Believe that there is safety, goodness, and love. You may be surprised."

"The Cat Ship will be here soon," Mukti informed them as he scanned a timetable. "If we hurry, we should be able to board."

Seal gave Prajna one last hug, then they departed to the street where the cormorants' bicycle rickshaw awaited. The group of friends held on tightly as Zochi pedaled with all his might. Speeding away through the streets of Kyoto, they headed toward the clearing where the Cat Ship would be arriving at any moment.

CHAPTER 16

THE PUNJAB

As they pulled up, the Cat Ship was loading final passengers. Mukti and Seal said a quick goodbye to the cormorants, then ran to the ship. Moments later, they took flight. Seal looked over the railing as their friends, Kyoto, and Japan fell further and further behind.

"Where's your *taus*, Seal?" Mukti asked, noticing its absence for the first time.

Hanging her head, Seal told Mukti of its brutal destruction. "I feel like I've lost an arm. It was becoming part of me…" Her voice trailed off.

"You lost it in a worthy effort," Mukti replied.

But her heart ached as she remembered Tansen giving it to her, back when her journey was just beginning. She wondered if she would ever see his beautiful, scraggly, ancient face again.

Seal's eyes grew heavy as she watched Mukti poring over his maps. Her body slouched, and her eyes were burning with weariness, but she forced herself to stay awake.

After a few hours, she began pacing the deck. *What I really want to do is ask Mukti about the next destination.* But he had sunken into a deep sleep. All she could do was wait and wonder.

As she glanced around at the other passengers, she noticed many of them were of dark complexion. Most had dark eyes as well, but occasionally, an animal with piercing green or hazel eyes would gaze at her. Many of them also sported long beards and various head coverings.

Finally, the Cat Ship descended onto a landing dock. Mukti casually yawned and stretched. It was completely dark outside. Seal was curious about where they were, but the landscape remained a mystery.

Exiting the ship, they continued forward and were soon part of a large crowd of pedestrians. Mukti pushed forward with certainty, and Seal hurried to keep pace. Unfamiliar languages were being spoken all around them. Brightly colored clothing swished. Scarves were blowing in the breeze. They made their way out of the crowd and through a series of small, winding streets.

Eventually, Mukti stopped at an iron door decorated with cheerful metal shapes in vivid colors. A whimsical lantern hung above it, spreading a welcoming glow, and to the side there was a sign that read, "The Inn of All Faiths."

"What does that mean?" Seal asked, gesturing toward the sign.

"This inn is dedicated to believers of every religion," he replied cheerfully. "Each room is decorated with art from different spiritual paths. It's a celebration of diversity." He punctuated the sentence with a florid gesture. "But," Mukti continued in a serious tone, "cats usually aren't allowed. So stay back a little and do your best to look harmless."

"I *am* harmless," Seal protested.

Mukti didn't respond but proceeded to knock loudly on the iron door. After several long moments, they heard movement from inside. A heavy lock clanked three times as a key was turned, then the door slowly opened, revealing a giant brown rat—almost as big as Seal. It eyed her suspiciously.

"She's okay, Nasir. Let us in. We need a place to stay until morning."

"Only for you, my friend," the rat replied, stepping aside.

Nasir led them down a dim, lamplit hall. The mustard-colored walls were lined with fabric-framed thangka paintings. *It's like Tansen's monastery.* She smiled in recognition. Opening a door, the large rat motioned for them to enter. *It's so pretty!* Seal thought. There was a large statue of Buddha on a table near the window, and the walls were covered with beautiful paintings lit by lanterns hanging above them. Large, plump cushions dotted the floor. The room felt warm, safe, and beautiful.

Seal pointed to one of the paintings, which showed a large elephant with a small rat at his feet.

"Ganesha, remover of obstacles," Mukti informed her.

"And this one?" Seal pointed to the figure of a blue man playing a flute in a forest.

"Krishna," Mukti whispered in reverence.

Seal gaped as she paused in front of another portrait. This one showed a different blue man with a trident.

"Shiva!" the mouse said with a grin.

The last picture on that wall was of a beautiful woman seated on a lotus flower in a pool of water. There were elephants on either side of her, spraying water into the air. Seal pointed to it.

"Lakshmi!" Mukti happily told her.

On the opposite wall hung another set of paintings showing some bearded men.

"What about these?" Seal asked.

"Ahhh," Mukti mused. "The Gurus…"

One portrait was of a dignified, turbaned man with

a falcon. "Guru Gobind Singh," Mukti announced. Another wore a different style of turban and had a great white beard. He nodded to it. "Guru Nanak."

Seal stopped in front of a painting that showed a turbaned man with a long, dark beard, sitting in a chamber. On one side of him was a cloth-covered book, and on the other side, a window looked out upon a lovely golden building surrounded by water.

"I know this place! Ardaas and I were there when we met the bearded man who gave us the fragrant tulsi leaves. That was many lifetimes ago… Is it still there?" she eagerly asked the little mouse.

He looked triumphant. "That's Guru Ram Das. Yes, that place sure is still there! It's called the Golden Temple. We're going there first thing tomorrow."

Seal lay down to rest, her heart lighter than it had been in a long time. The prospect of revisiting this special place felt like medicine for her soul.

CHAPTER 17

THE GOLDEN TEMPLE

Nasir's Inn of All Faiths proved to be a peaceful haven for the travelers. Seal slept quickly and deeply. Before she knew it, she was being startled into wakefulness from the sensation of Mukti poking her in the side. It was still completely dark outside.

"It's time to get up, Seal," he whispered.

"Why?" she complained. "It's still dark." She curled up tighter on her cushion and peeked out at the mouse from under her paw.

He went over to a mirror, carrying his bundle of special cloth from Prajna, and expertly began wrapping it around his head until it made a smart-looking turban. Then he began his morning yoga stretches and exercises. Next, he sat down with his spine straight, taking quick breaths through his nose. Finally, he grew totally still. His little legs were bent into lotus posture, and his eyes were narrowed to slits.

Seal was still tired from the journey, so she rested a bit longer as she watched her friend. Mukti was breathing slow, his beard waving with each exhale. Curiosity got the better of her again. *The beard...is it fake?* She began creeping toward him. Mukti didn't move. As she got closer, she reached out.

Just as her paw was hovering over the beard, Mukti's eyes snapped open. He gave her a stern look, then ordered, "Get dressed!"

"Yes, sir!" she replied as she retreated back.

Seal took the snowy cloth from her travel pouch and studied it. She tried to remember how Mukti had wrapped his. After struggling with it in front of the mirror for a while, she turned around, sporting something that looked more like a bird's nest gone wrong than a turban.

Mukti laughed. "Like this," he said, demonstrating with his tiny paws.

Seal tried again with some improvement, but the result was still terrible.

"I'm going back to my meditation," Mukti said. "Do it until you get it right."

Seal sighed and began again. Fifteen minutes later, she was still struggling. She felt like her arms were going to fall off. "I give up, Mukti. I can't do it. It's still a mess."

Mukti's eyes opened slowly. "Two more minutes! Concentrate—become the cloth."

Become the cloth? Seal thought. *Mukti is getting pretty weird.*

Taking a deep breath, she started again. This time, Seal moved slowly, focusing at her brow. She wound the cloth carefully, sensing where it should go. Her muscles ached terribly, and she wanted nothing more than to put the fabric down and forget about it. But there was another part of her. It felt expansive and like it could go on tying the turban forever. How could that be? These two feelings existing in the same self, and at the same time? Focusing on the space between the two thoughts, Seal became absorbed in the gap and kept moving.

"Huzzah!" Mukti suddenly burst out. "You did it!"

Seal looked in the mirror. Her reflection showed a very smart turban swaddled about her head. It was quite becoming and brought a grin to her face. "I did it!"

"Just in time too," Mukti said. "We'd better hurry or we'll be late."

"Late for what?" Seal asked.

Without answering, Mukti whisked out the door,

down the hall, and out into the street, with Seal scurrying behind.

It was pitch dark, and the streets were deserted. The two friends wound their way to and fro, and every now and then, Seal felt eyes staring out from dim alleyways. Was that the scent of gorillas in the entry they'd just passed? It faded too quickly to be certain.

More pedestrians began to appear, all heading in the same direction. The men sported turbans and were mostly bearded. They wore long tunics that swished as they walked. Some of the women had turbans as well, but most wore beautiful sheer scarves of every hue imaginable, which floated on the breeze. Everyone's clothing was made of brightly colored and embroidered fabrics. They reminded Seal of flowers in a field. She and Mukti were now part of a crowd that hurried along the dark streets like a living river.

They continued on until they came to a small building that had green metal benches before it. One side of the structure was open, with a countertop running its length.

"Everyone working in there is a volunteer," Mukti informed her.

Looking over the counter, Seal saw many rows of tall, compartmented shelves. Most of the cubbies were filled with shoes. *It looks like a library of footwear.*

Sitting down on one of the benches, the friends removed their shoes. Immediately after Seal placed the shoes on the counter, a volunteer plucked them up and disappeared down an aisle. After a few moments, he returned and handed Seal a flat metal token with Punjabi numbers stamped across it.

"Keep that safe, Seal. That's the only way we'll get our shoes back!" Mukti told her.

Opening her travel pouch, she dropped the token snugly inside.

They turned and continued along a wide marble walkway. Toward the end of it was a little depression full of clear water.

"We wash our feet in here," Mukti explained.

Standing in the warm, shallow pool, they shuffled their feet to get any loose dirt off, then stepped out and continued forward, descending a long flight of cold marble steps.

The sound of a horn greeted their ears, and soon she saw a palanquin carried by many men and women. A low square shape covered in beautifully embroidered cloths and strung with garlands of flowers sat atop it.

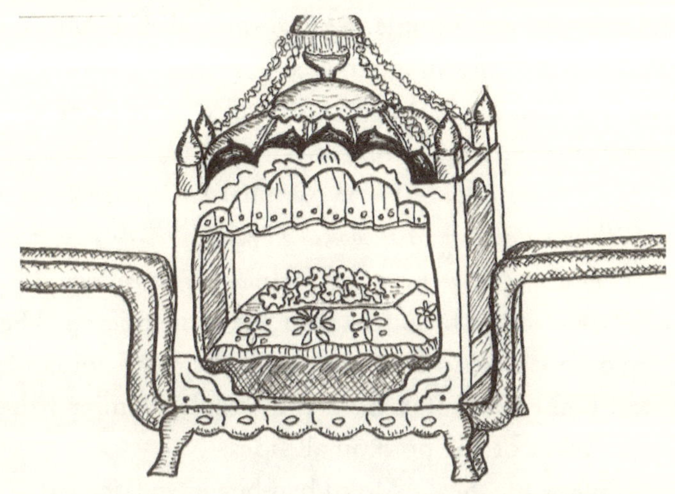

"Mukti," Seal asked in awe. "What are they carrying?"

"It's the Sri Guru Granth Sahib or 'Guru,' " he explained. "The Sikh scriptures are treated respectfully—as if they are a living holy person."

Seal watched as bystanders chanted and threw flower petals toward the Guru, just as if they were showering a royal person with them. "This is an interesting place," she whispered.

"Yes, it is!" Mukti answered. "Holy saints and people meditated here long before the Sikh Gurus came."

The procession was now passing in front of them. Everyone began bowing their foreheads to the ground in respect, then rose after the Guru had passed.

The Guru was carried through an open marble gateway and across a causeway that stretched toward the center of a great pool of water. At the end of it was the Golden Temple. Seal gasped in awe. She inhaled the cold morning air as she watched the procession disappearing through the small central door into the sanctuary of the temple.

Seal was amazed at how familiar this place felt to her. *It's just the same as it looked in my vision. In some past life, I stood in this very spot with Ardaas,* she reflected in awe. It was more beautiful than she remembered. The temple appeared to be floating like a gilded lotus on water. Light and color from the temple illumined the gentle waves of the pool on all sides.

"Follow me, Seal." Mukti had begun walking off to the left of the gateway.

"Aren't we going to go inside?" she asked, concerned. She really wanted to see what was going on in there.

"Absolutely!" the mouse chimed. "But first, we have to prepare ourselves."

They continued around the sacred pool. Gazing down as she moved, she noticed that the white marble was laced with geometric patterns and stripes of black and gold. It was beautiful but chilled her feet. All along the water's edge were stairs leading down into the shimmering waves. Here and there, men and boys in shorts were gathered around the sides, bathing.

"This is called *ishnaan*, Seal," Mukti informed her as he started disrobing down to his tiny trunks. "That's what we call bathing in the sacred water, before we go inside the temple. There's a special private bath house for girls over there." He pointed with his little pink

paw to the farther side of the water. "It's under that special tree."

"Why is the tree special?"

His eyes widened in enthusiasm as he explained, "The tree's called Dukh Bhanjani. It's a ber fruit tree, and scholars believe it is over four hundred years old! Legend says that in ancient times, when wild tulsi still grew along the shore, a great miracle of healing happened there." He grinned, then turned and carefully waded down into the sacred water to begin his *ishnaan*.

Seal continued walking in the direction Mukti had indicated. Rounding the far corner of the sacred pool, she soon came to a small structure hugging the water's edge that was built around the base of the special tree. Part of the building was a small temple, and there was a glass window where she could see another cloth-covered Guru was placed reverently. To the side was a doorway that led into the ladies' bath house

Seal entered and hung her clothing on one of the many hooks lining the wall. Slowly, she went down the steps toward the water. Huge orange, black, and white fish were swimming gracefully below. Her eyes darted this way and that, watching them as they glided through the emerald pool. As soon as her paws touched the water's surface, the fish sensed her and swam away. She was sad to see them go.

The water felt cold and invigorating. After a few moments, she worked up enough courage to go in further, moving forward until more than half her body was submerged. Seal watched the other bathers dipping themselves up and down in the water several times before getting out. She followed their example. When her *ishnaan* was complete, she climbed out and shook herself dry. She was shivering and hurried to get dressed.

Mukti was already waiting for her when she emerged from the exit. He smiled, and they continued around the walkway. Eventually, they found themselves back at the gate house, which led to the temple in the center of the sacred pool.

Seal noticed the *Ik Onkar* symbol on lanterns along the causeway. *Divine force in everything,* she thought.

They had to wait in a long line as they inched toward the temple door. Looking down, she noticed the colored stones had been cut into delicate shapes of graceful swimming fish. The sacred site seemed to marry earth and sky together. The temple felt like a portal for people of all faiths to experience the energy of the Divine.

When they reached the doorway, Mukti bowed his forehead to the threshold. Seal followed his example. Inside, there was a box for offerings, and they both dropped coins inside. The Siri Guru Granth Sahib was now before them, placed under a large, elaborately embroidered canopy and covered in matching cloths. Mukti and Seal bowed in front of it.

As they stood up, Seal let her eyes take everything in. The floor in front of the Guru was decorated with shiny pieces of armor. Spears, swords, shields, and some large metal rings she had never seen before. A large, artful arrangement of hundreds of fresh flowers had been lain out, and more blooms had been strung into long garlands that hung from the ceiling in swags. Seal took a deep breath. *The temple smells so fresh and sweet.*

The other visitors were wearing clothing and symbols from many different religions. Some had Hindu tilak marks or bindi dots on their foreheads. Others wore Muslim caps. In one corner were a group of Buddhist monks with shaved heads, wearing burgundy and saffron robes. Many looked like tourists from far, distant lands. All were welcome—all were equal. All were enjoying the unique spiritual vibrations of the surroundings.

The temple itself was one of the most beautiful places Seal had ever seen. Intricate golden panels embossed with floral designs lined the walls and ceiling. The floor was of colorful, patterned marble. A huge crystal chandelier hung in the center. It seemed to reflect and amplify the golden glow of the room.

A group of musicians were situated to the left of the Guru. They now began chanting. Seal's heart filled with joy. "Music!" she whispered to Mukti.

"Wouldn't be the Golden Temple without it!" he replied with a twinkle in his eyes. "Sacred music is played here all day long. Each group plays for about an hour and then a new group comes to take over."

Seal closed her eyes. The sound pulsed through her. When she opened them again, she noticed a black, bearded cat in a dark blue turban beckoning to them from across the temple. She and Mukti made their way over and followed him up a narrow spiral staircase. The milky-white steps had been worn down from the passing of thousands of feet.

Upstairs, the walls were painstakingly painted with colorful designs of scrolling leaves, flowers, and animals. One panel had a yogi in the center with white elephants on either side of him. The ceiling was covered in a tapestry of jewel tones and dotted with mirrored circles. It gave the effect of glittering stars in a fantastic sky.

The second floor formed a sort of balcony over the first. Visitors were clustered around the edges, where they could look down to the level below. Everyone was listening to the music or reading prayer books. There was a feeling of peace and protection in the air. *If only I could get Ardaas here, he would be safe*, she mused.

The dark cat turned with a white, pointy-toothed smile and motioned for them to follow once again. Up another flight of winding marble stairs, they emerged on the rooftop into cold, fresh air.

CHAPTER 18

BLESSINGS

THE SKY WAS BEGINNING TO FILL WITH COLORS OF RICH salmon, green, and blue. It made the entire temple and surrounding water shimmer. Seal deeply inhaled the crisp morning air. They walked a little way across the smooth bricks that had been lain out in geometric patterns of red and black.

"Even the rooftop is beautiful!" Seal whispered to Mukti.

He looked up and smiled in agreement.

Their new companion turned to them. "Sat Sri Akal!" he spoke the traditional Sikh greeting. "I'm Niyama. Tansen asked me to help you during your time here."

They made their way over to the edge of the roof and surveyed the temple complex. Many buildings and some towers were visible.

Niyama motioned to the water. "The *Sarovar*."

Seal smiled, gazing out over the gentle waves. "*Sarovar*… It's amazing!"

They turned to look at the roof, where the dome of the temple arose in the center. Glancing over at Mukti, Seal suddenly remembered the afternoon he had come to get her at the orphanage. It seemed so long ago, almost like another lifetime. She felt like a completely different cat. How far she had come! How far was there still to go?

From inside the dome, the voice of a woman could be heard, reading the sacred texts of the Siri Guru Granth Sahib. Seal's ears perked up. The language had a musical beauty to it. She heard rhythm and poetry in the words, and even though she didn't understand them, she felt her soul knew what they expressed.

The three companions continued walking around the rooftop. As they descended the spiral stairs back into the temple, Seal was greeted with the most unexpected, familiar sound—a *taus*. Hurrying to the edge of the balcony, she promptly sat down. Mukti and Niyama followed, and they clustered in together.

A new group of musicians was seated near the Guru. The highly skilled men and women were playing different instruments and chanting. The voice of the *taus* vibrated the air with its delicate song.

"I didn't know it was Indian!" Seal whispered excitedly. She was curious about the other instruments being played. Poking Niyama, she whispered, "What are those?"

"Ahhh, the jatha." He smiled. "The center one is playing the harmonium—it's a small organ that sits directly on the floor. Left of that are the tabla drums. To the right of the harmonium is a *taus*. Behind that is the rabab—kind of like a guitar. Behind them is the tanpura. The tanpura strings play a sort of droning sound that sets the background for every other note."

The music continued swelling the temple with magnificent, haunting sounds. Seal's eyes narrowed, and a swoon-like trance came over her. The notes vibrated through every cell of her being. It felt like nectar was being poured in through the top of her head. Her breathing slowed, and her attention focused on the utter stillness of her body. She no longer saw, and she didn't hear. She just was. She was in a gap. In the dark, she began to see an orb, blue and bright, floating before her eyes. Then she heard a voice. It was Ardaas.

"I'm still here, Seal. Please help!"

The orb faded and was replaced by the image of a dimly lit room. The smell of gorilla was strong. Ardaas's wicker prison was lying on its side on a trash-strewn table. She sensed his energy was fading. Perhaps he'd been hurt in her last attempt to save him. Looking around, she saw Kadir lying motionless on the floor, asleep. The guard apes were lingering over the remnants of their last meal.

Seal felt like her soul was rising out of the gloomy room now, through the ceiling. Farther and farther up she went. Now she could see the outside of the building. It was a little, mud-colored cottage. The roof was made of stone slabs, and a large, straggled tree was growing near a wall that enclosed the house within a small courtyard.

Up into the sky, Seal's soul floated. The surrounding landscape came into view. The house was situated in a forested mountain area. Far off on the horizon, Seal could see the jagged peaks of soaring snowcaps. Now it felt like she was being sucked up into the clouds, leaving the world beneath her behind.

Her eyes snapped open. The sounds of the temple music flooded her again. She sat puzzled, wondering what had just happened. Anxious to tell Mukti about what she had just seen, she turned to him but realized she would have to wait.

The mouse, with closed eyes, was chanting along with the sublime music. His beard waggled away as he repeated the holy *Shabads* with passion and devotion. He looked completely in his element.

The sun was now high in the sky.

Niyama stood up. "Follow me," he said with a grin.

They reluctantly left the temple. As they exited the causeway, volunteers plopped something warm and sweet-smelling into their cupped paws. Seal sniffed eagerly at the fragrant, greasy lumps.

"It's *prashad*, Seal." Niyama smiled as he popped his into his mouth. "It is a blessing."

Taking small, deliberate bites, Seal ate hers, then licked the remaining oil from her paws.

"Come on, let's go to the *langar*," Niyama said.

"What's the *langar*?" Seal asked, wondering what other surprises the temple had to offer.

"It's the fulfillment of Guru's wish. Men, women, and children; rich and poor; and followers of all religions sit down together to share a meal. No distinction, no discrimination. All are one," he explained, smiling. "The temple provides food every day, for free."

"Wow!" Seal's eyes widened. As they hurried along to keep pace with their guide, she scanned the crowd. Many visitors were regular-looking, like her and Mukti, while some were crippled, ill, or looked very poor. "For some of these people, this is a huge blessing," she whispered.

Niyama turned, nodding silently in agreement.

The clatter from the *langar* hall was deafening as they approached. Hundreds of individuals were milling about, doing various jobs. Some were distributing metal trays, bowls, and spoons. Dozens were sitting on the ground peeling garlic, shelling peas, and chopping vegetables. Some were serving tea. Seal, Mukti, and Niyama each received a tray, shallow bowl, and a spoon and were directed to follow the crowd of people around the side of the tall, red-brick building.

Inside the large hall rang with the sounds of many voices. Strips of burlap cloth for sitting spanned the length of the room, with large open aisles between the rows. The three companions joined a line on the far side of the room and sat down.

"Soon volunteers called *sevadars* will come with food," Niyama said as they placed their trays on the floor in front of them.

The *sevadars* began moving up and down the aisles. Some ladled out portions of curry from huge metal buckets. One was passing out warm roti bread from a large flat basket, and another served savory rice. Finally, a volunteer came around with a container of rich, creamy rice pudding with slivers of almonds, coconut, and raisins in it. Seal's mouth watered as she watched a huge ladleful being poured onto her tray.

"It's called *kheer*," Niyama joyfully explained.

"This place feels so healing and good! The Siri Guru Granth Sahib, the music, the temple, the *Sarovar*, *prashad*, and now a meal," she said in between large spoonfuls of the delicious pudding. It was so warm, sweet, and thick. Next, she tore little pieces of her roti bread and used them to scoop curry and rice into her awaiting mouth.

Beside her, Mukti was savoring his curry. It was *sarson ka saag*, made with mustard leaves and cubes of paneer cheese. His beard was becoming dotted with little specks of green sauce.

The water-dispensing volunteer soon appeared, and Seal watched him with delight. He was using handles to steer a huge barrel on wheels. They also had a system of handbrakes, like on a bicycle, that made the spigot near the bottom open or close. Seal smiled as a stream of water poured forth from it, filling her metal bowl. Then, releasing the handles to close the spigot, the *sevadar* wheeled off to the next bowl.

The companions were finishing the last morsels on their trays when Niyama cheerfully said, "Let's go help clean." They got up and crossed an open walkway to another part of the building complex.

The din in the cleanup area was almost unbearable. Tin trays, spoons, and bowls clashed together violently as they were washed in large troughs. Others were slinging the clean dishes into huge holding carts to dry. Seal and Niyama started loading bins with clean trays while Mukti perched on one of the sinks. He scrubbed the bowls in a frenzied manner, sudsy water splashing everywhere. The three companions laughed and smiled as they worked.

An hour later, exhausted but glowing, they left their jobs.

"Come with me," Niyama said. "You'll be staying in my home while you are in Amritsar."

CHAPTER 19

PICKING UP THE TRAIL

THEY WALKED BACK TO WHERE THEIR SHOES HAD BEEN stored. Seal handed a woman at the counter her metal token, and moments later their shoes were plopped on the countertop.

Mukti and Seal followed Niyama down a narrow street that coiled like a snake around the perimeter of the temple complex. Large trees overhead created a pleasant shade in the afternoon heat.

Finally, by a little shop where dough was being fried into large puffy circles, they turned right onto a side street. A few moments later, Niyama disappeared. He had quickly turned into a narrow walkway between two pink buildings. Seal paused. She was afraid to follow—it was such a strange, deserted little alley. But Mukti trotted after the dark cat with confidence. *It must be okay,* she figured and hurried to catch up.

The buildings were so tall that no sunshine reached the small, dead-end street. Doorways lined both sides of it. Some of the houses had balconies on their second floors that looked out into the tiny space. *Not much of a view*, Seal thought. The pavement was broken in many places, and there was a thin carpet of slimy moss where a constant stream of water crossed it. Seal's nose wrinkled as she passed.

At the very end of the alley, Niyama stopped and unlatched a door. Seal looked up. There was a large cement *Ik Onkar* shape above the doorway.

The three of them stepped inside the dark, cold house and followed Niyama up a steep, narrow staircase. Seal was amazed at the difference on the second floor. Sunshine angled through the windows on this level, making the large room bright. The floors were covered in colorful patterned tiles. She trilled, surveying the room. *It's really quite charming*. She smiled, inhaling deeply. The space was clean, and a cool draft made it fresh.

Niyama pulled aside a cotton curtain with a cheerful print and gestured to the room behind it. "You can rest here."

Seal chose a thick, floral cushion that lay in a sunny corner and tucked her head under her paw.

Mukti climbed up the side of a blanket to rest on the big bed opposite her.

"While you rest, I'll go collect your things from Nasir's place," Niyama said. "I should return within the hour."

Seal was truly exhausted. Although it was only late afternoon, it felt like many days had passed since morning. She closed her eyes and lay still but didn't fall asleep. Her tail twitched, and she listened to the sound of her breath.

After a long while, the door latch clanked below, and she could hear Niyama's footsteps coming up the stairs.

Seal lay awhile longer, then sat up, looking around the room. Mukti was sprawled out on the covers, snoring now and then. Her ears turned as they caught a new sound. Faint noises like musical notes were coming from far off. Sliding off her cushion, she crept out of the room and followed the sound up another flight of stairs. At the top, she emerged onto a sunny roof terrace. It was a pleasant open space full of plants, which made her forget she was in a busy city. Niyama was at the far end under some large potted trees.

"He's tuning a *taus!*" Seal whispered to herself in amazement. Standing unseen in the doorway, she enjoyed the beautiful scene. Niyama seemed like he had a wonderful heart, and he was also quite handsome. When he was near her or looked deeply into her eyes, something of that old feeling returned—the sensation that somehow everything was perfect, exactly as it was.

When the tuning was complete, Niyama looked up and saw Seal. She blushed, then hurried over.

Niyama smiled as Seal sat down next to him.

"What a beautiful instrument," she whispered in soft tones. The *taus* was made of the finest wood. It was decorated with delicate mother-of-pearl designs depicting scrolls, flowers, and animals. Springy, bright green-and-blue peacock feathers sprouted from the back.

"I didn't know you played *taus*, Niyama!"

"I don't play this one." He grinned, his teeth glinting through his black beard. "My instruments are over there."

Seal looked toward where he gestured. She saw a tanpura and something he told her was called a sitar on a blanket under another shady tree.

"This *taus* is for you." Niyama held it out to her. "A gift from your friends…"

It was so beautiful. Seal was almost afraid to touch it.

"Come, let's play," he said gently.

Niyama took up his tanpura, and began moving his paw across the strings, releasing a magical, undulating drone. Picking up her bow, Seal began playing. The voice of the *taus* came to life, and the two instruments began speaking in the ancient language of sound vibrations.

Song filled the air, rising and falling like a musical wind, then faded out. The sun had moved lower, painting the sky in rich violets and deep oranges.

They laid their instruments carefully aside, then Niyama reached into a small basket. He handed Seal a small mango and then took one for himself. The sky's colors deepened as they ate the sweet fruit.

"So what's next?" Niyama asked as they licked the juice from their paws. "Do you know where to go?"

Seal recalled what she had seen during her vision in the temple that morning. "I saw a stone cottage. A high-walled courtyard surrounded by forest and snow-capped mountains. How do I find Ardaas from that?"

Niyama grinned. "You traveled there today, didn't you?"

Seal was surprised. "Yes," she whispered. "But how do you know?"

Niyama ignored her question and continued, "Well, let's go again and get more clues. Seems the best way! Don't be afraid. Calmness will allow you to see much. Fear will pull you back."

Seal studied the dark cat. There were strange realities to this Universe she didn't understand, but Niyama seemed to have some knowledge of these secrets. She felt safe talking with him openly.

"When I was in Kyoto," she said quietly, "I began playing my *taus* when the gorillas were near. Something about it made them stop completely…"

"The power of the *naad*," Niyama whispered. "Music isn't a machine, Seal. It has power and secrets inside of it." He appeared to think for a few moments, then added, "I have a feeling the *naad* will help again before this is finished."

"What is *naad?*" she asked, puzzled once again.

"The essence of sound," he whispered.

Seal positioned the bow over her *taus* as Niyama resumed running his paw over the stings of his tanpura.

Just then, Mukti appeared, yawning in the doorway. He'd heard the music and come up with a tiny set of tabla drums in his arms. Sitting down with his friends, he used a little hammer to hit the wooden pegs strapped to the sides of the drums, bringing them to pitch. They had a surprisingly full and deep tone, just like a normal-sized set. Once his adjustments were complete, Mukti began playing in earnest. The drums burst to life with the unmistakable, unique voice of tabla.

The trio created a wave of sound that carried them along.

Seal concentrated as the *naad*, the vibration of the sound current, moved through her, and a humid breeze rustled her fur. She felt her body steady on the ground, holding the *taus*, but a feeling of buoyancy was rising in her. Her awareness began to rise above her body. She was now looking down, watching herself playing with Niyama and Mukti below.

Her soul-self rose higher and higher and began to soar in the twilight sky. She looked at rivers and tried to make note of the landmarks she saw—anything that would help guide her. She etched it all in her memory as best she could. Then, once again, she found herself looking down upon the mud cottage.

Kadir was there, charging and careening about the courtyard, searching for something. Seal wondered if he sensed that her energy was near. The gorilla shouted angry cries to the guards, who also began looking around.

Just then, one excitedly clutched at a white mound that was in a corner, behind a stack of baskets. Kadir ran over and grabbed the fluffy shape. It was just a dirty wad of wool. His rage seemed to deepen, and a maniacal roar burst from him as he shredded it into tiny pieces. His head swung from side to side, and a fierce glare flashed in his eyes.

Seal remembered Niyama's instructions to be calm. *I need to see as much as I can.* But then, Kadir stopped dead, throwing his head back to look straight up in her direction. *Can he see me?* Her fear grew and she felt her soul-self being sucked back into the sky.

No! I have to get more information to save Ardaas. Focusing, she took slow breaths, trying to let the fear pass. It seemed like Kadir was looking straight at her. His nostrils flared, and his mighty chest heaved. Seal continued hovering, frozen. The ape's head rolled back as he gave another roar, then he returned to his frantic search. It seemed she had been sensed but not seen.

Hovering around the building, Seal took in every detail. There was a window next to the door, but it had bars over it. Guard apes were stationed both in the small courtyard and outside the main gate. There was one other small window that jutted out from a gable in the roof, and it was open. On the opposite side of the house, one of the scraggled tree's branches came close to the wall's edge.

This may be the only way, Seal thought.

Kadir was still charging around. Again, he centered himself directly under Seal's soul-self. He became a mad cyclone of fur and rage. Lunging far up into the sky, his teeth gnashed, and his primal roar thundered. Seal felt terror as his great arms reached forward, his hands clawing as if to tear her from the sky.

Her face crinkled as she closed her eyes, waiting to feel the crushing strength of his fingers. Instead, they passed through air. Kadir crashed back to the ground, empty-handed. The tension and fear were too much for Seal now. She felt a snap like a soap bubble popping and was back in her body on the roof terrace.

The music abruptly stopped. Mukti hurried over to Seal, while Niyama grabbed hold of the *taus* just as it was falling from her grasp. All her strength had vanished, and a soft cry came from her as she slumped forward.

Niyama helped her back up, and he and Mukti sat quietly, waiting for her to speak.

Concentrating, Seal focused, trying to recall everything she had just experienced. As the moon was rising, she told them what she had seen on her spiritual journey.

Mukti began taking notes about everything she remembered. "Let me get all this down. These are great clues, Seal." He scribbled details about the landscape and cottage. "Now, help me draw a map of the locations you saw."

"The great thing is"—Niyama's eyes sparkled as he spoke—"gorillas are not native to India, and Kadir doesn't live quietly. So, if we wait just a little, we're bound to hear reports about where he's hiding out." He gave them a satisfied smile.

Seal felt troubled and agitated. She paced for some time before sitting down, watching as strips of clouds sped across the sky, blacking out the moon as they crossed its full, round face. Ardaas was still in danger. There was no way of knowing if he was hurt. Maybe too much time had gone by since her last attempt to save him.

Mukti's pencil eventually stopped moving, and he slumped down into a deep slumber.

Niyama was across the terrace from Seal, his bright amber eyes the only thing indicating where he was.

She was weary and felt a sickness in the pit of her stomach. Wandering over to the edge of the terrace, she looked down into the empty street below. Some rats scurried in the shadows, and a stray dog was sleeping on the neighbor's doorstep.

Life is vast, she thought. *Sometimes I feel so afraid.*

She glanced back to where Niyama's eyes were glowing. He disappeared completely when he blinked.

More clouds floated by, and the moon disappeared again. Dark, black, deep.

A sob escaped Seal as she gazed into the night. Her paw brushed away a few stray tears as she went back into the house to lie down. "Hopefully, tomorrow I'll feel better," she whispered to herself as she sank down onto a soft cushion.

CHAPTER 20

WAITING AND AN UNEXPECTED GUEST

MORNING BROKE WITH DIM, SILVER SKIES AND THUNDER. Niyama was in the kitchen, rustling up special Indian pancakes.

Mukti had put on his waterproof coat and cap. "I'm heading out to do some scouting, Seal. I have some ideas about where Kadir might be hiding," he said while strapping on his travel pack.

"Can't I come too?" she pleaded with hopeful eyes.

"It's best for you to stay put until I've located Kadir's new hideout. He has a network of spies who will be on the lookout for you, but not for me." The mouse's beard lifted as he grinned.

"How long will you be gone?"

"Not sure. Maybe a couple days. Maybe a couple months. Depends on how good my guesses are, and how willing people are to talk."

Seal's face sank at the idea of months possibly passing before Mukti's return. Her stomach was doing summersaults, and her heart felt heavy with a sense of urgency, mystery, and dread. *Ardaas needs to be found—quickly.*

"Is there anything I can do to help while you're gone?" she asked anxiously.

Mukti smiled. "Keep practicing your skills, and take time to go into the silence."

Seal sadly nodded, feeling useless.

Her friend whistled as he walked out. She stared at the door a few moments after he had gone, then went to find Niyama in the kitchen.

"Gooooood morning, Seal," he said with a pointy-toothed grin. He was holding out a plate of pancakes for her.

She couldn't help but smile at his kindness. "Thank you, Niyama." Taking the plate, she sat down near the kitchen window. She wasn't hungry but managed to chew the savory pancakes in her dry mouth.

Rain was pattering down outside. Little rivers streamed down the alley and out into the main road.

Niyama came and sat beside Seal, handing her a little red mug of Indian spiced milk tea. They gazed out the kitchen window as water fell endlessly from the sky. Reaching over, he grasped Seal's paw and held it. She felt a buzzing sensation, like some energy current or silent communication was flowing between them.

Time disappeared, but for perhaps an hour, they sat like this.

Finally, it felt like the current had finished flowing. Niyama moved his paw away and smiled.

As she looked at him, Seal realized that she wasn't feeling as troubled.

"How is your mind, Seal?" the dark cat asked, looking deeply into her eyes.

Seal thought a moment before answering, "I feel a sense of peace—that, as strange and uncertain as things are, somehow it's all okay. Things are as they should be."

Niyama smiled at her, then got up to make them another cup of tea.

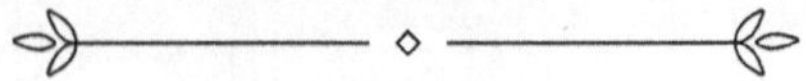

Days and weeks crept by without her hearing anything from Mukti. Seal grew more and more worried about his safety. A nervous agitation filled her thoughts and made her body restless. *Maybe I should have insisted on going with him. He was right about one thing though—Mukti will be almost invisible to Kadir, the guard apes, or any spies.* Then she tried to be positive. *Perhaps he's found the new hideout and will be back soon.*

Every morning, Seal sat in silence. Most days, there were only scattered, quiet thoughts. When they did get noisier, she noticed that they had taken on the quality of dreams. The thoughts sounded like nonsense babbling. It was as if the sentences and ideas had reverted into a big soup, with no meaning at all. Seal quietly observed this, then listened to the sound of her breath, letting the babble flow away.

There was a routine to her days. After eating breakfast, she would help Niyama clean up. When her food had settled, she would head up to the terrace for a few hours to work on her soto technique. Seal practiced in the rain and on the hottest days, so as to gain skill and endurance. In the evenings, she would play her *taus* while Niyama accompanied her on one of his instruments. Often, before sunrise and sometimes at night after dinner, they would walk together to the Golden Temple to sit and help serve.

Then late one afternoon, while they were preparing afternoon tea, a loud banging came from the door below.

"Seal, will you get that?" Niyama asked.

Looking at him, she felt puzzled.

A playful sparkle had come into his eyes, and it seemed like he was trying not to smile. "We have a guest coming to stay with us for a while, and I believe he's just arrived!"

Maybe Mukti has returned! she thought hopefully. Carefully, she crept down the dark, steep stairs to the bottom floor. A set of green windows cast an eerie glow through the unused sitting room. It felt like a cave compared to the sunny upper rooms.

Unlatching the door, Seal opened it with a clank. There stood a figure with his back to her, swaddled head to foot in saffron-and-rust-colored robes. Slowly, the visitor turned and gave Seal the most mischievous smile.

Her mouth dropped open, and she froze, unable to speak. Finally, one word escaped her, in a tone soft with amazement and disbelief.

"Tansen."

Tansen, her beloved first teacher. Somehow here he was! She looked up at his familiar face. The dark eyes, straggled whiskers, and wrinkles looked just as she remembered.

He grabbed Seal's shoulders firmly, eyes glowing with joy and wet with tears, pulling her into a strong embrace.

Seal's own cheeks were soaked as she nestled her head into Tansen's chest.

Just then, Niyama's voice called down from above, "Tea's ready! Come on up!"

Seal and Tansen gazed into each other's eyes for a few moments, then headed upstairs.

CHAPTER 21

THE SECRET SPY

TANSEN, SEAL, AND NIYAMA SAT IN THE BRIGHT UP-
stairs room, sipping their sweet tea.

The ancient cat dipped a third biscuit into his cup
with a smile, then munched it noisily. After the dishes
had been cleared away, he took up his travel bag and
removed a small bundle of cloth. Holding it out to

Seal, he said, "I've brought you your robe from the monastery. It was looking very lonely without you." He chuckled. "Go ahead and put it on."

She took it and buried her nose in the folds, inhaling. The fabric was saturated with the fragrance of incense and marigolds. "It smells just like the temple," she whispered. How could she have imagined this unexpected joy? She had feared she might never see Tansen again. Now, here he was, next to her. Seal left the room and quickly reappeared in her little saffron-and-rust-colored robe.

Now Tansen looked at her in all seriousness. "It's time to begin your advanced training," he said. "While Mukti is gone, we have just a little time to work."

More training? What could it be? she wondered, feeling her stomach tighten in fear. Then, smiling at her dear teacher, she reached out and hugged him again. *I won't worry, I'll just be happy,* she decided.

"Tomorrow we'll begin," he concluded, a slow smile spreading across his face.

Seal awoke early the next morning, had breakfast as usual, then went to find Tansen.

He was in the large sitting room with the floral tiles, meditating. His eyes were narrowed into the thinnest of slivers, and he sat straight and completely still.

Seal wasn't sure what to do. *It's best not to disturb him. But what about the important advanced training that there isn't much time to complete?* Quietly, she sat down near him to wait. *Maybe he'll be done soon.*

Seal sat, and sat, and sat. Tansen didn't move.

After almost an hour had passed, she decided it

might be best to continue her regular daily routine. Careful not to disturb her teacher, she stood and made her way up to the roof terrace to begin her practice.

As soon as Seal had left the room, Tansen's eyes popped open. He had been waiting for her to leave. Quietly he tiptoed to the doorway and watched as she disappeared up the stairs to the roof. He waited several moments, then quickly followed her. If anyone had seen him, they would have said he looked exactly like a naughty child who was up to some trick.

When he got to the doorway, he opened it just enough to have a decent view but remain hidden.

Seal had already begun and was concentrating deeply on her maneuvers. Niyama had been making practice courses for her on the roof. He switched it up a bit every few days to challenge her. Today the course contained a pile of bricks, bars of iron, shards of glass, boards with nails, a plastic sheet made slippery with water, and obstacles of old wooden furniture.

Tansen watched eagerly as Seal made her way through the course. She was having difficulty moving through the wet plastic area. Her paws kept sliding in all four directions, and she repeatedly slammed into the hurdle that came after. Again and again she tried. Her focus didn't fail. All the while, her teacher watched intently.

Finally, after a few hours, she was able to complete the course perfectly. Panting, she padded off to rest under the potted trees.

The old cat smiled, then swiftly and silently returned to the room below.

When Seal came back downstairs, she stopped at the sitting-room door. Tansen was still meditating. *He hasn't moved at all!* she thought in disbelief. Quietly, she went to the kitchen to sit with Niyama near the window.

Time passed, and Seal was feeling restless. *When will the advanced training begin?* she wondered impatiently.

She busied herself with helping Niyama make lunch. Today they were having South Indian–style food as a special treat—*uttapam*, *dosas*, spicy *sambar*, and coconut chutney.

When the food was ready, they carried it into the sitting room. Tansen was standing with his back to them, gazing out the window. *Finally, his meditation is over.* Seal sighed with relief.

She watched him steadily as they ate, itching to ask about the training, but he was concentrating on his meal. They munched on in silence, savoring the food until their bellies were full.

Afterward, she and Niyama removed the dishes and started cleaning the lunch mess in the kitchen. Seal hurriedly scrubbed all the dinnerware and cooking pans.

"I have to get back in there fast in case Tansen starts meditating again," she told Niyama as she hurriedly dried the trays and swept the vegetable peels from the floor.

The kitchen was cleaned in record time, but nonetheless, when Seal poked her head back into the sitting room, she found it completely empty. Where was Tansen? She crept up to the roof and peeked out.

There he was, under the trees. Again, he was in undisturbable, deep meditation. The corners of her mouth fell. Plopping herself down near him, she began to wait.

After a while, her body jerked. She had started falling asleep. Opening her eyes, she straightened herself. More time passed. Tansen hadn't moved a muscle. Once more, her eyelids started feeling heavy. *Maybe I should just continue with my regular routine. Apparently, there isn't going to be any advanced training this afternoon.* Seal sighed, then slinked off.

She padded back down to the sitting room. Taking her *taus* from the corner, she made herself comfortable on a stack of cushions. Music always made her feel better, and this time was no exception.

Softly, she began to play. A sound of longing came from the *taus*. Niyama appeared, arranging himself near her with his tanpura. He began plucking the strings, creating that magic drone that felt like the foundation of the Universe. The two musicians soon went very deep into their practice. The outside world disappeared.

Seal couldn't see it, but as soon as she had left the terrace, Tansen had popped one eye open to survey the scene. When he was convinced she wasn't coming back, he quickly and silently snuck down the stairs.

Chuckling to himself, he whispered, "I'm like a robber in the night, sneaking here and there."

By now, the sounds of Seal's *taus* were floating through the rooms of the house. The old cat crept toward the sitting-room door and pressed his ear close. He smiled widely, his eyes filling with a rare fire as he listened to the progress she had made.

As the final notes were just beginning to fade away, her eccentric teacher moved with stealth and agility, quickly returning to the roof terrace.

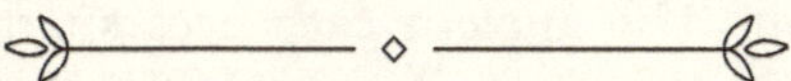

Seal carefully wrapped up her *taus* and put it away. "I am going to check on Tansen," she said to Niyama.

He bowed his head quietly, and gently smiled.

Tiptoeing back up to the terrace doorway, she peeked out. There he was. *He hasn't moved a muscle. This is some extreme meditation,* she thought. Never had she seen him sit for so long. *Perhaps it's in preparation for my advanced training,* she reasoned.

Several days passed much like the first. Seal would sit and meditate next to Tansen each morning. After an hour, she would wait to see if he would end his meditation and speak to her. But he just kept sitting. The only time she saw him come out of meditation was for meals. He didn't make any conversation while they were eating, and he never mentioned anything more about advanced training.

By this time, she had stopped waiting for him to talk to her. She just went about her normal routine and worked very diligently at her studies. She was a little sad, not because the advanced training didn't seem to be happening, but because her teacher was so quiet these days. She really missed his wise words and playful sense of humor.

Over the course of those several days, Tansen observed her keenly.

It had been months since her time at his mountaintop monastery. She'd only just begun her journey at that point. The ancient cat's eyes sparkled, and he smiled joyfully as he observed just how much she had grown. It was apparent that Seal was seriously committed to her studies. Every morning when they sat together in meditation, he could sense the deep inner stillness of her being. Later in the day, when she was exerting herself with soto technique, he observed her focus of mind and physical dedication. Regardless of the weather or how tired she was, she kept going until she had made a little more progress. During Seal's musical practice, Tansen listened intently and heard how she had gone deep into a relationship with the notes. The music wasn't just being played. It was like a living being that filled the room.

Once when Seal was still working through that day's obstacle course on the roof, Tansen bumped into Niyama on the stairs. Niyama was surprised to see him up and about. The mischievous teacher simply smiled at him with moist, cheerful eyes and whispered, "She's coming along very nicely!" Then he lifted a paw to his mouth and made a "Shhhhh" sound. Niyama understood he was not to tell Seal what her teacher had been up to.

Then one day, a couple weeks after Tansen's arrival, something unexpected happened. They had been sitting together in the pale morning light, meditating, when Seal got up to go about the rest of her daily routine as usual.

"Where do you think you're going?" her teacher called out with authority.

Seal froze.

"It's time to begin your advanced training."

CHAPTER 22

ADVANCED TRAINING

So the advanced training was to begin! Seal whirled around in delight and returned to Tansen's side, giving the ancient cat her complete attention.

"Now comes the most difficult part of your training, Seal," he said.

She fidgeted a bit, wondering what was coming.

Tansen continued in a low, direct voice, "Point number one. There is no person and no thing, outside of you, that can save you. Do you understand? No one else can do the work for you. Not even I can do that. Not even the greatest master."

"I think I understand," Seal murmured. "When I was facing Kadir in Kyoto, even though I had help getting there, ultimately I was alone." She felt tears welling up in her eyes. "I'm also alone when I sit in silence. Everything else falls away…"

"Remember, alone doesn't mean lonely," Tansen continued.

She realized this was very true. She had been alone

many times since kittenhood but hadn't felt lonely, just a deep sense of quiet.

"Point number two," Tansen went on. "It's important to know you can trust the guidance within you."

Seal recalled times in her past when listening to her intuition had been of some benefit or even saved her from harm.

"Point number three. You must be comfortable within yourself no matter what. If pain comes, if happiness comes. Whatever life puts before you"—his face had come very close to hers to emphasize his point—"meet it with your Buddha mind. In absolute peace and poise."

Seal tried to take in the meaning of his words.

"Point number four. What you are is eternal, beyond any passing changes. All difficulties that come to you have one thing in common—that they will go. Also good to remember is that the good times will pass. Everything is always flowing." He waved his arms like wings, demonstrating the flow. "But what *you* are is steady." He fell into silence, allowing time for his words to sink in. Then he finished enthusiastically, "So, now we begin!"

We haven't even begun yet? Seal felt overwhelmed. She was still trying to wrap her mind around points one through four.

"Sit up straight and become very still. Let your eyes close gently," Tansen instructed her. "Now, from ears to toes and toes to ears, feel every part of your body. Don't skip one inch."

Seal began noticing the sensation of her ears, her

face, her whiskers… Down she moved. Her hips felt tight from yesterday's soto practice, her foot pads felt cold…

"Notice every feeling in every part of you. Up and down, down and up. Don't forget your tail," he added with a chuckle.

Seal felt her tail. The tip of it was twitching.

So they continued. Periodically, Tansen would guide her awareness with his words, reminding her to keep her attention moving, noticing every feeling. "When you feel something nice, don't grab on to it. When you feel something unpleasant, don't grab on to it. Everything that comes, goes. Suffering results when you grasp either end."

Seal did her best to follow his instructions.

By the time they had finished, the sun was setting large and red in the sky.

She felt defeated, her body stiff and uncomfortable. "How is this advanced training going to help me save Ardaas?"

Tansen smiled. "When your mind listens to you, then great power is coming. It has started listening instead of talking. Kadir's mind only talks to him. You are gaining the ability to remain calm and detached in any situation. You have the advantage."

The next morning after breakfast, Tansen clapped his paws and rubbed them together, saying, "Now the difficult work begins. You're about to see how many tricks your mind can play on you. You have loosened its grip on your awareness. But the mind won't give up without a fight." He smiled mischievously.

"What kind of tricks? What will the fight be?" Seal asked.

"Unbelievable pain, fire, millions of biting ants!" Tansen's face jutted toward her. His voice was full of doom, and his dark eyes expanded with a strange intensity.

Seal inched backward. Maybe she didn't want this advanced training after all.

"You must remember, Seal. None of it is real. It's just the games of the mind." Her teacher had shrunk back to his normal self, his eyes soft and loving. "Try not to move. Stay still and see what happens. If you can face this side of your mind, you can conquer the world."

"Are you ready to begin?" he asked. "We will practice ten days of meditation, using the new scanning technique." He was looking at her, his gaze the most serious one she had ever seen.

She mirrored him, her eyes slightly narrowing in concentration, then gave a determined nod.

He returned her gesture. "Then let's begin!"

After just the first day, Seal realized she wouldn't be able to practice the obstacle courses or play her *taus* until the new training was complete. Hour after hour, day after day, she just sat with Tansen, practicing the new technique of observing the sensations in her body. They took short breaks after every hour of sitting. Niyama brought them meals of fruit and broth. Three times a day, they would walk on the roof, stretching and relaxing.

On the second day of training, Seal became disturbed by a pain between her shoulders. She couldn't think what it was. Hour after hour, it grew and burned until it felt like a great ball of fire in her back.

This is real! I have some problem with my muscles or spine. Maybe I'll get permanent damage if I keep sitting.

For three more days, the painful ball of fire continued and intensified, but then a curious thing happened. When the break chime rang, she noticed the horrible burning spot had completely vanished.

Wait a minute, how can that be? I haven't even shifted position or stood up yet... Hey, the ball of fire is a mind game! She narrowed her eyes with the new awareness of her mind's sneakiness.

When they sat again after the break, the ball of fire quickly returned. Seal sat feeling it, but with the new idea that it wasn't a real problem. Remaining still, she concentrated on noticing all of the other sensations in her body. Eventually, she was surprised to realize that

the burning pain had completely vanished. From that day onward, it never came back.

After the day's meditations were complete, Tansen would tell her interesting stories about the lives of spiritual masters or other beings traveling the path of meditation and inner wisdom. Sometimes he talked about when he was young, and his master was teaching him. The stories were always funny and made her laugh out loud. She was glad this training wasn't all work and no play.

Halfway through the training, Tansen sat with her in the candlelit meditation room and began a more serious talk. "Seal, it's time to face your fears. Everything that you've been running from your whole life."

I don't want to face them. She cringed. *I just want to feel good.* But then she thought about how it felt to run and feel like you were hiding from something. *It doesn't matter if it is inside or outside, no one can run from anything forever. I am afraid, but I can also be brave.* She stiffened her lip as she prepared for what was to come next.

As she sat, she became aware of her fears. "I used to be afraid of darkness. That's gone away." Now she loved lying in a completely dark room before going to sleep at night, looking into the emptiness. If there was no moon, the blackness was so complete that she couldn't tell if her eyes were open or closed. It felt magical and like the night was holding her in a loving way.

Now, she had a more unusual fear. It was of cold brightness. "The white light of day has an emptiness about it that sometimes fills me with terror. I can't explain it." Tansen nodded, then she continued, "I'm afraid of not being loved or wanted, and being a failure."

Then the dread of Kadir loomed up. His violence made her tremble. "I'm afraid of Kadir," she admitted. "And that I won't be able to save Ardaas." Tears welled up in her eyes, and her body shook with a deep sob that burst forth.

It was hard to acknowledge all of these things. But she sat with them, allowing them to be. Not running from them.

The following morning, Seal's meditations went by smooth and fast. They felt deep and wonderful, like swimming in vast outer space. During the afternoon break, she was happy, thinking about how easy the morning had been. She was looking forward to the second half of the day. But when Seal sat on her cushion after lunch, she quickly realized everything had changed.

She had begun in stillness, scanning her body, when a creepy sensation spread over her arms and legs. It seemed like itchy ants were crawling all over her. The feeling was so real, she couldn't resist opening her eyes. Shifting her robes this way and that, she checked her legs for the thousands of insects that must be there. Nothing. *It's another mind game!* Squeezing her eyes shut, Seal tried to pay attention to her breath and any other feelings in her body.

How come it's so hard to ignore something that isn't real? she wondered in frustration. Again, her eyes popped open, and she examined her fuzzy arms and legs. Now it felt like the ants were giving her stinging bites. She shifted, trying to inspect herself without Tansen noticing. There wasn't one ant, let alone thousands.

Inhaling deeply, she attempted to sit still again, but

before she knew it, she had given in. She was doing a sort of jig as she rubbed and scratched, trying to get some relief.

Tansen heard the commotion, and his eyes opened a sliver. Gazing sidelong at her, he shouted sternly, "Games!" Then his eyes snapped shut again.

After several more minutes, the chime finally rang, letting them know that the hour was up. Seal noticed the thousand ants were completely gone in one instant. *Games! How can my mind be so tricky and mean?* she thought.

Her teacher noticed her agitation. "Don't grab. Let it pass. Now you see what you're up against. Most people live their whole lives without really meeting their mind and seeing its games. Keep going, Seal. Keep going." His tone was loving. Shuffling his foot, he reached down to scratch it, then said with a chuckle. "Your mind ants are coming over here!"

After that, a few days passed without any incident. Then, on the last full day of meditation, Seal had a challenging morning. For the first couple hours, she felt excruciating pain in her whole body. This time, she stayed steady and breathed through it. After lunch, she was afraid to sit again. She still had several hours of meditation left. How could she possibly get through it?

Scanning her body, she sat waiting for the pain. But it was gone. Instead, she felt a warm flush of vibrating energy spreading through every cell. The crown of her head felt like it had a tingling openness. Breathing slowly and steadily, she remained aware of every sensation. Then she recalled Tansen's instructions not to grab on to any experience, even the good ones. She felt thankful for what she was feeling, but there was also a whisper in her mind, saying it was okay for the experience to pass. It was like how a beautiful wave of the ocean comes to the shore and then flows away again. Or how a breath comes into the body but also must go out again.

It doesn't make sense to grab on to or hold it. It has to go, but it might come back again someday. Like a beautiful sunset or the sweet smell of blossoms on the breeze. I can't hold on to any of those either, just enjoy them while they last.

And so the day ended, and her advanced training was completed.

They celebrated with a quiet dinner. Seal and Tansen both looked a bit bedraggled, and their eyes were hanging heavy. They decided it would be best to get to bed early. Niyama had freshened their sleeping areas that day. Seal's cushion had a clean, new cover that smelled like sunshine, and Tansen's bed sheets were crisp and cool. *I wonder what we'll do tomorrow, now that the training is complete,* Seal wondered as she drifted off to sleep.

CHAPTER 23

FRUITFUL RESULTS AND A VISION

SEAL'S EYES POPPED OPEN THE NEXT MORNING.

"Aagh!" she yelled. Her heart nearly stopped at the shock of seeing Tansen's face just inches from hers. His eyes were dark, shining pools, and his fur and whiskers were tousled in a funny way from sleep.

"You're awake!" He smiled. Then, sitting back up, he continued, "I'm feeling a craving for some fresh fruit. What do you think, shall we go to the market?"

Seal stretched and yawned. A market trip with Tansen. It really would be like old times.

There was no scooter for them to use here, so they just walked. Seal gazed up at her teacher as they made their way through the winding city streets. He took her paw in his as they wandered by a strange pack of street dogs, but he didn't drop it once they were past them. That made her very happy.

As they continued toward the fruit market, he asked, "What are you hungry for, Seal?"

She considered for a moment, then exclaimed,

"Mangos!" Her mouth began to water as she imagined the soft fruits, whose taste was like heavenly nectar.

Turning down a narrow lane, they passed under a gigantic banyan tree that erupted from a small temple in the middle of a tiny intersection. Its huge trunk emerged from the ground, and long limbs sprawled through the windows of the adjacent buildings. Seal and Tansen paused a moment in awe, staring at the unusual sight. Pedestrians and scooters navigated around it, as if it were perfectly normal to find a giant tree growing out of the road.

The ancient cat chuckled, "You can see everything in India."

Seal nodded.

Rounding the next corner, they came to a halt, frozen by an unexpected sight.

"Mukti!" they cried out in unison.

There he was, treading down the street toward them. As he came close, Seal could see that his clothes were dirty and torn. Brambles were stuck in his beard. He looked very tired but also happy.

"Tansen! Seal!" He scurried forward to meet them.

"We came out to get fruit," Seal explained as her teacher took Mukti's pack to ease his load. Seal bent down so that her friend could climb on her shoulder for a ride.

As they continued on their way, the mouse began telling them the findings of his scouting.

"I had to travel in three directions from Amritsar. Kadir has a large network of criminals in his service. He made sure that anyone asking about him would be given false leads." He looked down with regret. "The first two places I traveled to were mistakes. I got there only to find none of the details matched your vision. And the locals in those areas had never heard of or seen him." Mukti paused his story when they arrived at the market.

The street was lined from end to end with wheeled carts. Some of the fruit sellers had placed burning incense on their wagons to keep the pesky flies away from their produce. Seal's nose twitched pleasantly at the unusual scent. Each cart was heaped with fruits for sale. They stood looking at all the choices. It was a little overwhelming. There were the familiar fruits, like pineapples, oranges, bananas, and mangoes. Other carts held more unusual fruits that Seal didn't even know the names of.

"Mukti," Tansen asked, "what would refresh you most?"

Mukti surveyed the street. "Well, if it's not too much trouble, I would really love some papayas and guavas!" He licked his lips.

They made their way over to one of the carts.

The old cat expertly selected the best pieces of fruit. "Green mangoes for Seal. Papayas and guavas for Mukti. Let's take some pomegranates and bananas for Niyama, and I think I'll have a little of each." He smiled. "It's a celebration feast now, after all!"

Two large bags were packed full of ripe fruit, and Tansen paid the seller. Hefting one of the loads onto his shoulder, he motioned for Seal to grab the second bag.

As they started back the way they had come, Mukti resumed his story.

"The third try felt like magic. I hit a *goldmine* of real witnesses who had encountered Kadir recently. I had to travel a long way, but after some time, the landscape began to look exactly like your description, Seal." He looked triumphant. "And everywhere I stopped to ask, people had seen both Kadir and his guards. As I got closer, I had to go incognito, just in case, so I dressed up in camouflage to do surveillance." Radiant joy spread across the mouse's face. "Guess what, Seal?"

"What, Mukti?" she asked.

"While I was doing some undercover spy work at a village market, I saw one of the guard apes come in for supplies. One of the things he bought was a packet of hummingbird food." He grinned from ear to ear.

Seal's eyes filled with tears. "Then Ardaas is still alive!" she cheered.

"For now," Mukti said as his face began to droop. "The guard was fighting with the shop owner. He said the last packet of special food was bad. That the bird wasn't eating it…"

Seal could feel her heart sinking. Hopefully Ardaas could hang on just a little longer. She was so close to reaching him and finally saving him.

"I'll show you the maps I made when we get back to the house," Mukti concluded.

When they returned, they heard Niyama upstairs in the kitchen, preparing a special treat to go with the fruit.

Seal paraded in with Mukti on her shoulder, announcing, "Look what the cat dragged in."

The mouse grinned, and Niyama's smile lit up the room. "Mukti! Oh dear, you look like you have been through the jungle," he exclaimed.

"I have been." the bedraggled mouse sighed.

"Go take a bath and rest while we prepare the fruit," Tansen directed.

When everything was ready, the four of them gathered in the sitting room to enjoy their small banquet. After they were finished eating, Tansen accidentally let out a room-shaking belch, then chuckled.

When Mukti felt revived, he went to his travel pack and pulled out a series of maps. Everyone clustered in to look at them.

"I had to travel all the way out of Punjab to find Kadir's new hideout," he began to explain. "I took the train into a different state called Uttarakhand. Then I had to trek for some days in the wilderness. Kadir is hiding in the mountains near the Himalayas." Mukti looked around at the listeners' faces. "We have to pass through these remote areas to get there. It will be dangerous. Ape guards are stationed there." He traced his little paw over the map. "We can hide from them, if we're careful. But I found out Kadir has arranged a huge network for surveillance and spying." He pointed to the large, forested areas that both led up to the hideout and surrounded it. "This is all jungle, inhabited by small brown monkeys and larger gray-and-black primates called langurs. As far as I could tell, many of the monkeys are working for Kadir. I am not certain about the langurs. They are very intelligent and tend to keep to themselves."

Niyama looked serious. "It will be a challenge, but I think it's possible to get to the hideout undetected," he said optimistically.

Seal's whole body contracted in fear. She had never been in the Indian jungle. It sounded scary. She also didn't like the idea of monkeys and langurs spying on them or coming after them.

Tansen listened calmly to the facts. He would not be going along, since he had to return to his duties at the monastery. "It is my dearest hope that this time you will finally be able to free Ardaas. My prayers and blessings for success are with you all." His words vibrated with emotion.

Mukti pulled out a second, more detailed map. "This is the most direct yet unobservable route. We can take the train to this point marked with a star. But from there, we are on foot. The train leaves at five-thirty tomorrow morning, and it will take ten hours to get to the end of the line. We'll still have several days of foot trekking after that."

When Mukti finished explaining the situation, everyone fell into a somber silence.

Finally, Tansen's cheerful voice broke the tension. "This plan seems good," he continued. "Thank you for all your work to prepare the way, Mukti. I think traveling under cover of darkness will be safest. Move only at night whenever possible, dear friends."

The serious look on Tansen's face doesn't match his happy tone, Seal observed uneasily.

The room was again filled with a silence that felt very grave. "Well, let's begin packing for the journey," Niyama said. "Then we should try to get some rest."

When their preparations were complete, Niyama lay down on a large, puffy cushion. Mukti climbed up on the bed near Tansen, and Seal lay near the open window. As she rested, her mind flooded with worries of the future and painful memories that arose like ghosts.

Maybe I'll fail again, and we'll have to track down another hideout. Or what if it takes us too long to get through the jungle to find Ardaas? Mukti heard the guard saying he wasn't eating. What if he's already... But no, she couldn't think like that. It didn't do any good.

Niyama was now sleeping soundly, his mouth agape. Mukti's beard quavered slightly as his breath came long and deep. His little round body turned as he shifted from one side to the other. Tansen was lying motionless on his back, with his hands clasped over his chest.

Seal felt wide awake. *I think I'll meditate. It might help me calm down so I can sleep.* Sitting up, she straightened her spine and slowed her breath until it almost seemed to stop. A great silence arose from within her. After her meditation was complete, a vision began to unfold.

A land of deep jungle appeared before her. Towering trees, thick bushes, and vines in many shades of green were growing all around. There was a small clearing where the vegetation opened into a grassy patch, with views of blue sky and billowing clouds overhead.

Seal watched as a tiny, dark shape galloped out of the dense forest, laughing. It was a baby gorilla. A large gorilla followed, calling out happily, "My little Kadir! Come back to your mama. It is time for your nap." Kadir's mother caught him and began tickling him. He rolled around in the grass, giggling, until she stopped. Then he sighed in relief.

Seal observed in amazement. *How could this sweet little thing be Kadir? What could have made him grow to become so bitter, angry, and horrible?* she wondered.

The vision shifted—time had passed. Kadir was still small but had grown. He was playing in the grassy clearing, and something was cradled in his arms. It was a small, fluffy kitten with orange-and-cream fur. The tiny ape was so happy. Seal could tell that these two were inseparable companions. He called out, "Ardaas! Ardaas! Come, jump on my shoulders." The little kitten hopped up. Then Kadir grabbed a long vine, and the two swung up into the treetops with a shout of joy.

Time shifted again. Kadir was playing with other little apes, swinging from vines and pounding their chests in a playful way. Ardaas was scampering along the tree branches, playing along as best he could.

Then, suddenly, Kadir's mother's voice called out anxiously, "Kadir, Kadir! Where are you? Come quickly!"

Ardaas jumped into his arms. The small apes looked at each other with fear, then hurried down from their treetop playground and ran to see what was wrong. The little gorilla lagged behind. He was still quite a bit smaller than the others. The group of friends came toward the clearing, where their families were huddled together. Some humans had surrounded them. Seal watched the vision as Kadir's friends emerged into the open grass and were quickly snatched up by the men.

She saw that Kadir was still hidden in the shadows of the jungle. He seemed to want to run to his mother, but she was motioning to him to stay where he was. A terrible look of fear was on his mother's face. Kadir wore a pained expression. Seal sensed that he was fighting with himself to stay hidden. He shifted back and forth several times, then charged out into view, yelling angrily. Seeing him, one of the men laughed cruelly, then forcefully snatched Ardaas from his arms.

No! Horror filled Seal as she watched the past unfold. Kadir was standing there stunned. She could tell he didn't understand what the human had done. When Ardaas was dropped back to the ground, his spine was strangely twisted, and he didn't move any more. Kadir looked at Ardaas sadly, and tears rolled down his face. Then another man took the butt of a big gun and hit the little gorilla across the face.

Kadir lay there, motionless. The humans turned back to close in on the group of apes. While the men weren't looking, the little gorilla slowly crawled back into the jungle and hid under some low plants. Seal saw him crouching, crying softly in his hiding place as he watched what was happening. When the humans had finished, none of his tribe were left alive.

Seal knew what it was like to not have a family. She knew that the little gorilla's life would never be the same again.

Then the vision leaped forward some years. Kadir was now almost fully grown. She watched as he tore angrily through a grassy meadow. He came to an abrupt stop when he heard the sounds of cheerful playing up ahead. Creeping forward, he spied from behind a tree to see what the noise was. Two kittens were playing in the long grass—one orange and creamy, the other white and gray with a flame mark on its brow.

Seal's breath caught as she realized what she was witnessing. *Ardaas is in his next cat life, and I'm with him!*

Kadir was trembling with rage, and his eyes seemed filled with jealousy at the sight of them playing together. He sprung out of the trees, roaring and scaring the kittens. Then he snatched at Ardaas but couldn't get ahold. The terrified kittens scrambled away into the jungle. Kadir stood there looking after them, his nostrils flaring and his heart pounding.

The vision slowly faded away. Seal began to cry. Despite her fear of Kadir, she now felt a great compassion for him. "Why do so many bad things have to happen in this world?" she whispered to the great Divine. "Why?"

Seal still wasn't sleepy, so she got up and went to the washroom. *I guess it's a good time for Gyoki's ancient sleeping technique,* she thought as she turned on the tap and began filling a large plastic tub. Stepping into the cold water, she began to shiver. She stood in the icy liquid until her teeth chattered. Afterward, she quietly made her way back to her cushion. Lying down on her right side, she covered her right nostril with her paw. Breathing deeply, she blinked a few times. An extreme, achy weariness overtook her body. A few more moments and she felt like she was ten thousand pounds of weight sinking down, down into the darkness.

CHAPTER 24

THE FINAL JOURNEY BEGINS

"It's time, Seal." Niyama was at her side with a warm, glowing oil lamp.

Sitting up, Seal looked around, squinting. The clock on the wall read 4:30 a.m. They had woken up early to have plenty of time to walk to the train station.

Soon, everyone was ready. Tansen had his belongings gathered. He would be starting his journey back to the monastery. Mukti had his maps in hand and was carrying a lumpy bag, his tabla drums stowed on his back. Niyama and Seal had their instruments strapped on their backs as well, along with their travel packs.

"One last thing for you," Tansen said with a smile. He pulled out a pink cotton shawl and handed it to Seal. "Use it to cover up while you travel, so no one can see your face." He hugged Seal tightly several times. "Bless you, little one," he whispered, then kissed her forehead and both of her cheeks.

Seal smiled and mimicked his gesture, kissing his forehead and his cheeks above the whiskers.

"Whatever happens, everything will be exactly as it should be," Tansen said. His calm assurance made her feel a bit better.

They went down the narrow, dark staircase together one last time. Niyama bolted the door behind them. Then they walked down the small alley and out into the main street.

"We head this direction," Mukti said, pointing to the left fork in the road, the starting point of their journey.

"And I go that way," Tansen replied, pointing to the right fork, which led to where the Cat Ship would be docking later that morning.

Final hugs and blessings were given, and they parted ways. Mukti was frowning. Seal's eyes were pools of tears that silently spilled over now and then. Niyama's perpetual smile was gone. Instead, lines of worry creased his forehead.

The three travelers made their way through the dense city.

They walked down endless, silent streets until they finally came to the train station.

"I'll go inside the office to buy the tickets," Niyama said. Mukti and Seal waited for him in the shadows. When he returned, he simply said, "Platform Eleven."

Hoisting up their travel gear, they quickly headed over. As they sat waiting for the train, Seal arranged her new shawl like a hood so that her face was hidden deep within the folds.

Mukti sighed in relief when the train pulled up on

time. The announcement speaker had indicated that some of the trains were running three hours late.

The trio quickly boarded and found their seats. Seal disappeared further into her shawl. There weren't any monkey passengers yet, but Mukti had warned them that, as the train neared the mountains and jungle, many would start boarding.

The mouse was still a bit worn out. He had only just returned from his previous scouting journey. Climbing into the folds of Seal's shawl, he nestled into her lap and fell asleep almost at once.

Niyama was vigilant. He sat in the aisle seat, keeping watch.

Seal stayed awake for a few hours, until the swaying motion of the train began rocking her to sleep.

There was a nervous moment when the tea service started coming through the train car. The server was a monkey! There was no way of knowing if he was also a spy. He kept staring at Seal's hooded form as Niyama placed their order. "Two cups of tea and biscuits, please."

The monkey took the order but kept trying to talk to Seal. "Madam. Madam, please give your order." He stooped, trying to look beneath the shawl. "Madam." He kept demanding a response.

"I've placed the order," Niyama said firmly.

But the monkey kept getting closer to Seal. He wasn't stopping. "Madam!" he continued, as his paw reached out toward her shawl hood.

She could hardly breathe.

"The tea is ordered, and she's sleeping. Leave her

alone!" Niyama said angrily as he swatted the monkey away.

The server's eyes narrowed with suspicion and anger. Finally, he stomped off but kept looking over his shoulder as he moved along the train car.

Seal sat frozen in fear for a long while.

When the tea finally arrived, Niyama lifted Seal's shawl and slipped her tea and a few biscuits underneath it. Mukti crept out to share Niyama's.

By now, she was feeling hot and stifled in her fabric prison. After finishing her tea, Seal turned toward the window. In this position, she could open a bigger breathing hole and still remain unobserved.

The train ride lasted for several more hours. As Mukti had warned, the further they went, the more monkey passengers boarded.

"I am going to be so relieved to get off this train!" Niyama whispered to his companions.

It was too much strain to think about being trapped in this car with dozens of potential spies. Seal was curious to see a langur from a safe distance, though. She wanted to know what those reclusive primates were like. But no langur entered the train.

The tea monkey came around one final time during the journey. This time, Niyama and Seal both pretended to be asleep. The monkey stood staring at them for several moments, then stalked off.

Popping an eye open, Niyama made sure the monkey was gone. Then his ears perked up as an announcement began over the speaker. "Only two stations until our stop!" he whispered excitedly. "It will come quickly, so let's get ready."

The three travelers organized their gear, preparing for a speedy exit.

Before they knew it, the train had reached the end of the line. Seal and Niyama stood up as it slowed to a jerky stop.

"Let's go!" Niyama was first out the door.

Seal followed closely behind but was suddenly stopped. Someone had grabbed tightly onto her arm from behind. *Oh no, it's probably that monkey!* She couldn't see because of her shawl. The person was babbling in some language she didn't understand. Turning, Seal peeked out and saw it was a strange cat. His long hair was matted, his eyes were googly and he looked very dirty.

Niyama spoke to the cat in the same language while handing him some money, then pulled Seal safely off the train. "He's a beggar cat," Niyama explained. "He just wanted some help."

But she was still scared. When she had turned toward the poor cat, the tea monkey had been standing just a few meters behind him. He had seen Seal's face. And she saw the suspicious monkey's eyes narrow in recognition and hostility.

Niyama kept ahold of Seal's paw, expertly guiding her this way and that. Mukti rode hidden in her shawl as they zipped across the train platform. Dozens of monkeys were perched above them on the rafters of the platform roof. They darted between passengers, trunks, and people sleeping on the ground as they headed for the exit.

Finally, they reached the door, which opened onto a small road. Across the street, the land rose up into hills covered with green plants, flowers, and trees. This was a very different landscape than Amritsar.

Niyama guided them down the road to the left, until they were far enough away from the crowds to talk freely. "Mukti, where do we go now?" he asked.

The mouse crawled out of the shawl and reached into his pack for the appropriate map. "We continue on this road. It leads away from the town." He paused a moment as he put the paper back in his bag, then continued, "Remember, Tansen told us to travel by night for safety. So we just need to get to a place where we can rest until it's dark. The terrain is going to be difficult. We'll be weaving up and down, from valleys to mountains, as we wind our way closer and closer to Kadir," he explained.

They continued on until the buildings became sparse and gave way to fields that were surrounded by thick jungle. There were strange tall trees here and there, which had gigantic maroon flower pods hanging from them.

"What are those trees with the huge, drooping blossoms?" Seal asked Niyama in awe.

"Those are banana trees," he replied with joy.

They walked to the edge of a field, where some thick bushes were clustered. "Let's take our rest here," Niyama suggested. Mukti and Seal agreed.

Climbing between the bushes, they found a flat

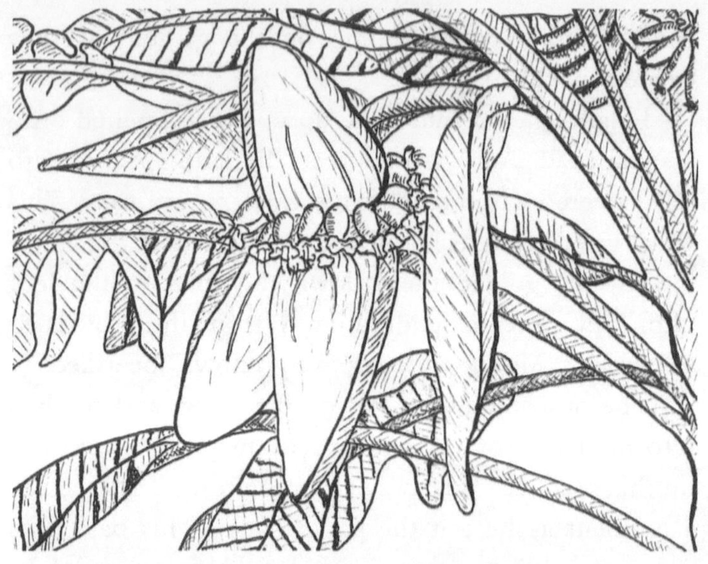

spot and used dried grass to make nests. Here they could remain hidden until dark.

The friends were able to sleep for about five hours, waking as the shadows of night fell. The temperature had dropped noticeably, and noises from strange insects and animals could be heard coming from the depths of the jungle. Stretching and yawning, the three companions huddled close together, waiting until all sounds of travelers on the road had subsided. When it seemed the coast was clear, they emerged and started their first night's journey.

Several hours later, their feet ached from walking, and one of Seal's back claws felt infected after snagging on some wild brush. Niyama was dehydrated and felt sick to his stomach. Luckily, Mukti was in better shape because he was able to ride on his companions.

As the first glow of daylight crept into the sky, they

found a place to stop. They made their way into a tight grove of trees, far from the road. Slouching to the ground with weariness, they began opening their packs. Niyama took out some cheese, and Seal handed out three pieces of fruit. The companions quickly ate, then lay down. It wasn't long before they were fast asleep.

The sun was warm that day and made their shady covering comfortable. In the late afternoon, a breeze rustled the forest leaves, bringing a pleasant coolness and sweet smells.

When the sun left the sky and the road was silent, the three travelers awoke and emerged from their hiding spot. Mukti checked the map, and they set off again.

The route began to twist. Winding dirt roads trailed on and on.

As dawn approached, they passed through a remote village. On the outskirts, a sugarcane field gave way to wild land.

"Let's take shelter here." Niyama suggested.

They entered the cane forest a little way and sat together. Seal opened a packet of nuts, and Niyama set out some fruit.

After eating, the three curled up near each other.

Seal whispered to her companions, "I haven't seen any monkeys or langurs yet."

"No," Mukti whispered back, "but we have to be vigilant. They move around a lot, so you never know where they might be in the jungle. Monkeys aren't so active at night, and we're hidden sleeping during the day, so that's lucky for us."

"We'll take all the luck we can get," Niyama added.

The trio slept deeply for a few hours. But by late morning, ominous black rain clouds had rolled in. The travelers bolted awake as the crash of thunder sounded.

"A storm is coming!" Niyama warned them. An icy wind was gaining speed. "This is going to be bad. Let's try to find shelter. Quickly!"

The friends ran out from the cane field and found an old woodshed near the road. They were just safely inside when a torrential downpour started.

Mukti sighed in relief. "We can stay dry in here until the storm clears."

Huddling together, they sat shivering under a piece of burlap.

Night eventually arrived, and the rain hadn't let up.

"We're going to have to stay here," Niyama said sadly.

Seal's face drooped.

During the night, Seal was awakened by a sound. She saw a mysterious yellow glow through the dirty window of the shed. Someone was moving about outside.

She quickly adjusted the burlap bag so that it covered her white shape more completely. Just her eyes were peeking out. Niyama was naturally camouflaged with his black fur, and the only thing visible on Mukti would have been his beard, but he was well hidden under the cloth. Seal stayed perfectly still as the brightness drew nearer and nearer.

Rain was pelting the glass, but when the light stopped just outside the window, she could see the face of a brown monkey. It was spookily lit from below by the lantern he held. The corners of his mouth were turned down in a sour expression. The spy's eyes shifted from side to side, as he searched. *I'm glad the rain was so strong—any footprints outside will have washed away by now*, she thought optimistically. Then, holding her breath, she sat waiting anxiously. But the monkey didn't leave. He had grabbed the doorknob and started turning it.

Niyama's eyes flashed open at the sound.

"Shhhh!" Seal whispered.

Mukti was peeking out from under the cloth, with a concerned look on his face.

The door slowly creaked open. Seal was afraid the sound of her heart pounding would give them away.

Stepping inside the doorway, the monkey lifted his lantern and scanned the floor. Then he stooped to pick something up.

What did he find? Seal thought fearfully.

The monkey didn't have time to look further, be-cause just then a forceful voice sounded from outside.

"Hey, you get out of there! You've been lurking around here too often. You're nothing but trouble. Get away—now!"

The monkey dropped his lantern outside the shed and ran off into the darkness.

Now a different form stood in the doorway. It was thin and tall. It would have towered over the brown monkey. Whitish-gray fur covered its body and long tail. Its black face peeked out from a ring of whitish fur. *A langur!* Seal thought. He picked up the lantern and casually looked inside. Seeming to find everything in order, he closed the door and went on his way.

Needless to say, for the rest of the night, there was no sleep for the three friends. They did their best to lie still as the rain poured down, but everyone was afraid of the monkey returning. After a long while, they began to whisper in the dark, discussing how they might attempt to stun Kadir and his guards with their music.

"If it worked in Nijo Castle, I think it will work again," Niyama said confidently.

But Seal was worried. "What if the apes are now immune to the hypnotic sounds?"

Mukti looked thoughtful but didn't give any opinion.

"Well, it's the only thing we've got for defense," Seal said. "We're no match for a troop of giant, angry gorillas."

Her companions nodded in agreement, then became quiet and fell into a slumber.

The morning dawned, dark and gloomy, as the rain continued pouring down relentlessly. Outside the shed, the winds howled, and the sugarcanes in the field beat together like war drums.

Finally, by evening the storm had passed. The sky was becoming sprinkled with stars.

"We should leave soon," Niyama said. "That creepy monkey might come back tonight."

The travelers took a small meal of crackers and dried fruit, then ventured out to continue their journey toward Kadir's hideout. Seal's and Niyama's paws squished and slid on the muddy road, making their progress slow. They continued on through the night under a moonless sky.

Pausing, Seal looked up to find one of her favorite constellations, Orion. The stars making up his sword seemed to be blinking sequentially, like a string of moving Christmas lights. Large banks of clouds periodically sailed swiftly overhead, like ships on a dark ocean.

She thought about Ardaas. "I hope he's still alive and okay," she whispered to the stars. Then she remembered Aisawa-san and Mi-chan on the farm in Japan and Tansen up in the Himalayas. *I hope I'll be able to see them all again someday.*

After hours and hours of walking, the horizon began to glow faintly.

"It's time to find a place to rest," Mukti said. "We still have quite a way to go until we reach the hideout."

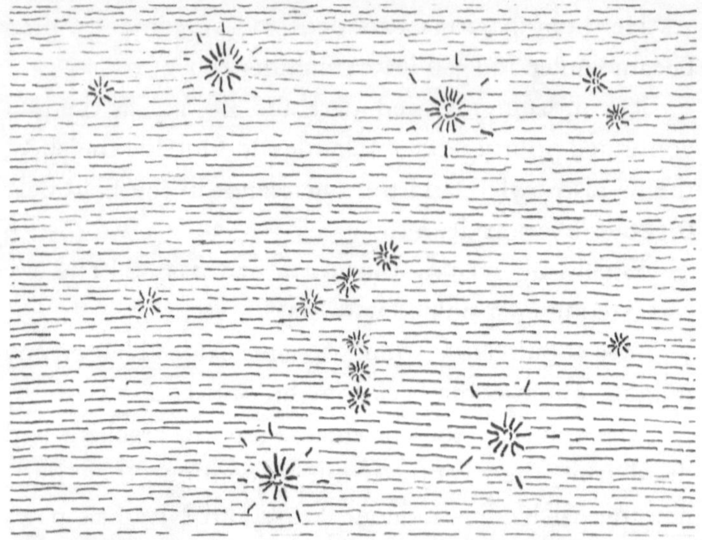

Seal's and Niyama's faces fell into frowns, and they sighed.

Over the next two days, the three travelers wound their way higher and higher into the remote mountain territory. Other than physical fatigue, the time passed uneventfully. They had reached terrain where there were no structures, just open stretches of tall lemongrass that grew thickly along terraced hills. As Seal paused to survey the road ahead, she saw that, toward the horizon, the grassland gave way once more to thick jungle.

Day was beginning to inch into the sky. Looking for their next resting spot, the travelers waded through the grass to a section that had grown extra thick and tall, then huddled inside it for cover.

Seal passed out hearty slices of buttered bread and

some dried fruit. They ate, then quickly fell into slumber. The sun continued to rise in the sky, warming their sleeping bodies. Soft winds blew, and Seal was vaguely aware of the sweet smells of the sunbaked grass as she dozed. But as the sky started to shift from late afternoon to the deeper blues of evening, her eyes snapped open with recognition at a very unwelcome scent on the wind. Gorilla.

"Mukti! Niyama!" she whispered. Their eyes popped open, and Seal put her paw up to her muzzle, motioning for them to remain silent. Raising her nose into the wind, she took several short sniffs. Niyama and Mukti followed suit, and everyone's face fell into expressions of fear. "I bet that monkey spy tipped them off. I saw him take something from the shed floor that night before he ran off."

Swishing and thudding sounds were now coming through the grass from several directions. The apes were searching the field.

"They're looking for us. They know we're here!" Seal whimpered.

Crouching down as low as they could, they could feel motions in the grass as the gorillas passed nearby.

Seal was trying to keep her body from shaking. She could hear grunting and breathing close by. A gorilla was heading straight for them.

"We have to run!" Mukti squeaked.

There was no time to think. They got up and ran. The grass was so tall it mostly hid them, but it also kept them from seeing where the apes were or where they were going. Seal felt terrified as she threaded her way through the grassland. Mukti had jumped onto Niyama's back and was holding on tight as they fled through the dim blue landscape.

Seal veered to the left, feeling the ground thundering as one of Kadir's scouts closed in on her. Looking behind, she saw the top of its head as it bounded closer and closer. A small cry escaped her, and she hurried on, zigzagging through the grass. Niyama and Mukti were no longer in sight. She prayed they would somehow be okay.

Seal was panting heavily and pushing herself as fast as she could, but the large ape was closing in on her. Panic filled her as she blazed through the twilight landscape.

Boom. The gorilla's fist crashed down to her right. She quickly barrel-rolled to the left. *Boom.* His fist came down to her left, barely missing her. She barrel-rolled

back to the right. *Thud.* Pain shot through her as his large hand seized her body, crushing it toward the earth. With all her effort, Seal elongated her spine and slipped through his grasp.

She shot through the grass like an arrow. Her heart was racing, and her lungs felt like they were going to burst. It seemed like time was moving in slow motion as her back paw caught on a twisted loop of old tree roots. Gravity pulled her to the ground with a thud. Her eyes were big and filled with fear as she lay there trembling, waiting for the weight of the gorilla to crush down upon her.

Swoosh, thud.

He passed over me. He didn't see me! She was still shaking as she began to crawl backward. The pounding of her heart was deafening.

A pale silver glow was now creeping over the landscape as the moon began to rise. Seal threaded her way back through the grass, moving farther and farther from the sounds of the giant apes.

After a long while, she finally came to a stop. All signs of the scouts had vanished. Sinking down, she sighed heavily.

Now she fretted. There were three big problems. First, she had no idea where she was. Second, she had no idea where Mukti and Niyama were. Third, her *taus* and travel bag weren't with her. In the scuffle, they had been left behind in the sea of grass.

Seal tried to think what to do. It wasn't long before her ears perked up. There was a faint, familiar sound in the distance. Then it stopped. She waited, ears alert.

The sound began again. She concentrated. *What is that?* she puzzled. Now it stopped.

After several moments, it started once more. *Dha-Gay Din Na—Dha-Gay Tin Na…*

Her ears moved like satellite dishes tuning in. *What is that sound? It's so familiar.* Her brow furrowed in concentration. It was the faint sound of tabla drums! She listened closely, but the rhythmic taps cut off unexpectedly.

The noise started up again. *It sounds like the drums are trying to talk in sentences instead of playing music.* Her head tilted attentively. *It must be Mukti. He's trying to let me know where he is!* Seal listened harder and started navigating in the direction of the tabla. *I hope he won't stop playing before I'm close enough to call out.*

Quickly, she trotted through the tall grass, only pausing when the drums became silent.

Finally, she felt close enough to venture making a sound. When the drumbeats paused, she took a deep breath, tilted her head up, and let out a long, low meow. Then, falling silent, she waited.

This time, the tabla replied with more force and speed. It didn't stop but kept a steady rhythm. Seal trotted toward it without stopping.

Pushing her nose through one last clump of thick grass, she came to an opening. There sat Mukti, pattering away with all his might. His brow was sweaty, and his sleeves were rolled up. Niyama was beside him, looking anxious. As Seal's white-and-gray face emerged through the sea of grass, her friends smiled in relief.

Mukti ended his drumming with a flamboyant flurry of taps, and they all sank to the ground.

Then Seal sighed. "I need to find my *taus*."

Niyama smiled. "There's a tree just a little way off. Let's climb it and see what we can see."

The three companions made their way over and climbed up. Sitting high in the branches, they surveyed the landscape. The lemongrass was parted in trails where the gorillas had passed through. Off to the north, a shadowy, dark mound was barely visible under the overarching grass.

"I think that's where we were sleeping before the scouts came," Niyama said as he pointed to the spot.

"Is that your *taus* hidden in the grass, or a gorilla?" Mukti asked with concern.

"We'll soon find out," Niyama replied.

Returning to the ground, they headed off in the direction of the shadow.

"We're close now," Mukti whispered. "Let me run ahead and check to be safe."

Seal and Niyama crouched low as he continued forward.

It seemed a long time before he returned. "It's the *taus*!" Mukti quietly cheered as he rejoined his friends.

With speed, Seal hurried over to collect her belongings. Luckily, everything was still intact.

Niyama sighed. "It's not fully dark yet, but I don't think it's safe to stay here any longer."

The others nodded in agreement.

"We also need to try to make up for lost time," Seal said.

They circled in close together while Mukti checked the maps and calibrated their direction. Then they set out, trying to remain as quiet as they could. There was no telling if gorillas or monkey spies might be lurking in the shadows.

For many hours, they traveled on and on until they saw daylight returning with a faint glow in the east. Leaving the road, the companions crept under some low-hanging brambles to rest. Too tired to eat anything, they collapsed into sleep.

CHAPTER 25

THE DEADLY ENCOUNTER

A COLD WIND HAD BEGUN TO HOWL WHEN THEY AWOKE for the next night's journey. Seal's fur flapped, her ears were low, and her eyes squinted as she battled through the gusts. Niyama's muzzle was blowing in the

wind, exposing his teeth. Mukti was riding in Niyama's travel pack so he wouldn't be blown away entirely.

Up and down hills, they forged their way on through wind-tossed darkness. The landscape had become wild and sinister. Seal felt frightened as shadows began to look like hunched apes in the darkness. There was a shrieking in the air. Was it the wind or spy monkeys announcing their presence?

They had entered a deep gorge. The road ran alongside a mostly dry riverbed with boulders and rocky banks. As the night was waning, they came to a bridge.

"Can we rest here?" Seal asked hopefully.

Niyama and Mukti looked around.

"It seems like it should be okay," Mukti replied.

Niyama nodded in agreement.

They settled into a crevice under the bridge, which would remain hidden during the day. Niyama passed around some crunchy biscuits. Seal was so tired her paw could barely lift the food to her mouth. They all curled up together when they had finished eating.

"Tonight we'll leave this valley and climb the winding road up the next mountain," Mukti said as they were drifting off to sleep. "If we can make good time, we should reach the hideout before morning."

This was good and bad news. They were all ready for this journey to end. But what would they face once they arrived at Kadir's lair?

"We need to arrive under cover of darkness." Mukti yawned. "There are too many…monkeys… and…gorillas…" Whistling snores were now the only sound coming from him.

Seal lay awake. *Soon I will face Kadir again*, she thought. *I'm afraid of the monkeys and guard apes. I don't know what will happen when I'm face to face with them.* Her thought train continued roaring on. *Is Ardaas still alive? Will I be able to save him this time? Am I already too late?* The sun had climbed high into the sky before she finally fell asleep.

Time passed quickly as the friends slumbered, and soon night fell once again. They woke, feeling the coolness of evening returning. The stars were shining as Mukti checked the map before they set out.

After several hours, the buildings of remote mountain villages began springing up here and there between long stretches of jungle. The roadside was bordered with bushes. Thorns littered the ground, scratching and painfully digging into their paws. The companions moved carefully, not wanting to wake anyone in the villages or look suspicious to any monkeys who might be sleeping in the trees overhead. They tried not to slow their pace or stop, since they had to reach the hideout before sunrise.

They traveled long and far, as the road looped up and around the mountain, climbing higher and higher. Then, a few hours after midnight, the unmistakable smell of gorillas grew thick in the air. Cautiously, they continued forward.

The moon cast enough light for them to see the outline of a building in the distance. As they came nearer, Seal recognized the stone cottage and courtyard. She noticed the scraggly tree outside the wall, which looked just as she had seen it in her soul's visit.

Several shadowy forms could be seen pacing the perimeter, guarding Kadir's lair.

The three friends hid in the shadowy jungle across the road from the cottage.

"I feel so tired," Seal whispered. "I don't know if I have the strength to do this."

Niyama and Mukti looked at her with love and understanding.

"I know." Mukti frowned, then his little face squeezed into a determined grin. "You can do it, Seal, and we'll do our best to help."

Niyama's smile and golden eyes shone through the darkness, and Seal's heart warmed with the support of her friends.

"Okay," she replied. "Let's begin."

They unpacked and readied their instruments. Niyama began a hypnotic drone by strumming his tanpura. Mukti joined in with rhythmic tapping on his tablas, then the voice-like notes of Seal's *taus* pierced the air.

A flurry of commotion moved through the shadowy treetops as a troop of monkeys became aware of their presence. Fearfully, Seal watched as several of them bounded toward the guard apes, communicating with them before disappearing into the depths of the jungle. Angry grunting could be heard—they had sounded the alarm.

Mukti, Seal, and Niyama kept their music going steadily as the gorillas came into a formation. One of the largest ones was out in front, giving some kind of orders, but soon, everything quieted down into a strange silence. The apes outside the compound walls had slumped down to the ground. They were in a deep trance.

"It's working!" Mukti said encouragingly.

The musicians inched forward as they continued playing. Kadir was inside the courtyard. They couldn't see him, but they could hear him moving. The music was only having a partial effect on him. There was still a sound of power, strength, and determination behind his motions as he searched for intruders.

A shudder passed through Seal as she heard his angry calls and violent movements inside the walls. It would still be a challenge to get past him.

"Let's take it up a notch," Mukti whispered. Then he put more intensity into his tabla.

Seal concentrated and tried to forget everything except the music.

Deeply haunting melodies poured forth from her *taus*. They continued playing as they listened for any movement within the courtyard. It sounded like Kadir was settling down. The guard apes outside the wall were completely tranquilized, and it seemed the monkeys had all fled the scene.

Now came the big risk. Seal would have to stop playing to continue her quest. Looking at her companions, she gave them a meaningful nod. With serious faces, her friends nodded back. Seal handed her *taus* to Niyama and he began playing the melody. Without looking back, she began soto technique to sneakily approach the hideout. The musicians redoubled their efforts to keep the guards asleep.

Sprinting to the tree near the courtyard wall, Seal quickly climbed to a great height. She made her way along an outstretched branch, which became thin and droopy as she edged toward its end. The courtyard wall was just ahead of her. There was only about six inches width to land on. She paused, calculating. *If I miss my mark, I'll either slam into the outside of the wall or skid off directly into Kadir's path.*

Seal focused her mind to center herself. Then, scootching down on the branch, she readied her stance and jumped. She landed on the wall with too much force. Her heart pounded as she hovered on the brink of falling. Once she was stable, she hurried along the top of the wall toward the side nearest the roof window.

Oh no! The window is tightly shut. Her mouth tightened as she considered her options. *I'll aim for the roof anyway.*

Then I will at least be inside the courtyard. After that, I can survey the scene below. Then she saw something that made her turn cold and tremble. She had been spotted.

The monkey spy who had come into the shed that rainy night was standing in front of Kadir. Seal watched as he handed the gorilla something small. It looked like a tuft of her white fur. Then the monkey turned with a sour look on his face and pointed up to where Seal was still perched. Kadir roared and began swinging forward toward her.

Seal only had seconds to prepare for the long leap—over three meters. Crouching to build momentum, she wiggled her hips. Her ears were pulled flat against her head.

Now! She leaped with all the force she could muster in that small space and flew through the air toward the roof. But it wasn't enough. Her front paws grabbed the edge, but too much of her weight was below the roofline. Her back legs pedaled into empty space. There was nothing to use to help herself up. Her claws couldn't gain traction on the slick stone roof tiles. She felt a terrifying feeling of slipping, then plummeted straight down.

Cats are lucky in many ways. They have an uncanny, instinctual ability to fall from heights and land gracefully on all four feet. Seal's spine elegantly twisted as she righted herself and prepared her paws for a safe landing. As soon as she hit the ground, she sped around the corner of the cottage, then darted under some rubbish piled against the wall.

The furious gorilla wasn't far behind. His head

swung back and forth in an angry effort to shake off the hypnotic stupor from the music. With wrath and determination, he rounded the back corner and stared a moment. Then, he began systematically swiping the rubbish away from the wall with deadly force.

Seal crouched low in the shadows. She could hear what was coming. Stealthily, she crept low to the ground under the cover of discarded wood, cloth, and garbage. She made it to the corner of the cottage and implemented soto technique, then reached the doorway.

Kadir hadn't seen her escape. His eyes were focused in front of him. He grew more and more angry as each swipe of his massive hand turned up nothing but emptiness under the trash. When he reached the end of the wall, he stood staring. The music seemed to be making his mind slow and unfocused. For some moments, he shuffled around the courtyard, checking under piles of baskets and heaps of cut grass.

Inside the cottage, Seal glanced around at the mud-colored walls and across the stone floor. The room was dimly lit by a small fireplace in one corner. Rubbish was scattered about, and the room stunk. It was a very gloomy scene.

Seal's heart caught in her throat as her eyes fell upon the small wicker prison lying sideways on a table. It was motionless. Was she too late? She quickly sprinted over, snatching up the handle in her mouth, and moved toward the firelight. After setting it down gently, she tried to peer inside.

"Ardaas!" she urgently whispered. "Are you in

there? Are you okay?" She stared intently at the little house.

Silence. Then after several moments, she heard Ardaas's voice. It sounded so quiet and weak she could barely hear it.

"Seal?"

She wanted to open the prison but was afraid she might hurt him if she jostled it too much. Under its roof edge, she felt a strongly knotted cord. Holding the wicker enclosure firmly between her back feet, she began working on the thin rope with her front claws and teeth. Finally, it slackened and fell, useless, to the ground. Opening the prison carefully, she looked inside.

Ardaas, weak from not eating and perhaps injured, was breathing shallowly and very slowly. His tiny eyes blinked as he gazed into the low glowing fire. After a few moments, he said with a quiet joy, "You found me, Seal! I knew you would…" Then his voice trailed off into stillness. Seal noticed his breathing was becoming more regular.

But the joy of their reunion was short-lived. Kadir's dark, massive form had appeared in the doorway. Angrily, he howled out a war call and stumbled in toward them.

Seal carefully slid Ardaas in his opened prison across the floor into the dark shadows to hide him.

The massive ape charged toward Seal. Now that they were face to face, the dark power of his jealousy and hatred were lessening the effects of the music. He was moving with more speed and accuracy. A look of evil spread across his face as he snarled, "I've got you where I want you! You will never see Ardaas again." Baring his teeth in a cruel smile, he continued, "This is the end."

Seal zigzagged, using all her well-practiced moves to avoid his grasp. She was near the doorway, but it was no good. *I can't leave without Ardaas. Not this time.*

Kadir's nostrils flared, and his muscular chest heaved. Seal trembled, looking at the cold, terrible giant. The ferocious glint in his dark eyes made her feel paralyzed.

I've got to get to Ardaas. Maybe I can trick Kadir. She started toward the opposite side of the room from where the bird was lying. Maybe this would keep him out of harm's way, she reasoned.

Focusing, she lowered herself, then started forward at lightning speed using her special maneuvers.

The gorilla's attention was divided. His eyes darted back and forth as he tried to track Seal and locate where Ardaas had been moved to. He was still under a slightly groggy haze that kept him from completely mastering the situation.

Seal circled back around the room. Her speed allowed her to launch up onto the walls as she rounded the dark corners. Stopping sharply, she abruptly took off in the opposite direction, again launching up onto the walls. Kadir was spinning as he tried to follow her movements.

Then, she saw her chance. The prison lay ahead of her. If she could just reach it and get to the door… It was only a few feet in front of her—she was almost there!

But the giant gorilla had guessed Seal's target and reached her in two strides. She halted as his form suddenly blocked the path to Ardaas.

For one moment their eyes locked, then they were both startled by a buzzing noise. Ardaas had gathered enough strength to fly. The little vibrating orb of his body was rising from the prison on the ground.

"Try to get away, Seal. Go!" he called out to her as he started moving toward them.

"Ardaas, no! Hide!" Seal called out desperately.

She tried to swerve around Kadir so she could stop him from coming any closer, but the ape's large hand reached out and grabbed her. This time, there was no *taus* on her back to take the brunt of his force. She heard a snap, and incredible pain shot through her body. Her legs went limp, and her mind became foggy.

She couldn't breathe. Her body thumped to the ground as Kadir released her. Seal lay in terrible pain, unable to move.

She watched fearfully as he readied a foot, as if to crush her. Then something strange happened. The massive ape stood there, looking down at Seal's body.

"Ardaas, no! What did they do to you?" he yelled out, then he began sobbing.

Seal was confused by his words. She watched as a change spread over his entire being and his body slackened. His eyes searchingly looked at her limp form, and all the rage had dropped from his face. Then Seal remembered the vision of little Kadir, when he had seen the humans kill his friend. She realized that her body now bore an uncanny resemblance to what Ardaas had looked like when he had fallen to the ground.

"Ardaas," the large ape quietly sobbed out the name. He gently lowered his foot back to the ground, then shook his head as if trying to clear away the images. His hands moved up to his head, and he let out a terrible roar of grief. Turning, he ran from the cottage and disappeared into the jungle.

By this time, Ardaas's energy gave way. He couldn't fly any longer. Gracefully, he glided down to Seal's side. "We're safe, Seal. We're safe," he whispered as he snuggled into her fur. Then he became very still. The strain had been too much. His tiny heart stopped.

The fire in the corner sputtered out, and darkness closed in completely.

CHAPTER 26

THE AFTERMATH

NIYAMA AND MUKTI LAID DOWN THEIR INSTRUMENTS and ran into the cottage as soon as Kadir fled the scene. Seal looked up at them wearily. Her friends looked down at her with great concern, then at each other.

Gazing out the doorway, Seal saw the guard apes coming out of their dreamlike trance. It seemed the prolonged exposure to the music had somehow freed their minds. After sitting for some moments, they began slowly and peacefully wandering off into the jungle.

"Look!" Mukti gasped as he noticed Ardaas's little form beside Seal.

Niyama bent forward and carefully placed his paw on the little bird. Then he looked at Mukti and shook his head sadly.

Mukti's head dropped, and a tear streamed down his face. "Seal?" he asked urgently.

"I can't move, Mukti," Seal labored to reply, her voice shaking from the pain racking her body. "Is Ardaas okay?"

He simply replied with fear in his voice, "We need to get help. Let's get out of here."

Niyama pulled part of his turban loose and ripped a small length of the fabric off to wrap the tiny hummingbird in. Then he placed the small body in his travel pack.

After Niyama hoisted Seal up into his arms, they set off down the forested road, returning from where they had come. The jungle wasn't nearly as sinister in the early morning light that was now creeping across the landscape. Lush ferns and moss dotted with delicate purple blossoms lined the roadside. The sky was transforming into a deep blue with honey-gold shafts spearing through the forest top. Friendly wads of clouds soared overhead. The air was scented with a sweet spiciness from the pine trees. It was all a strange contrast to the sad faces and hearts of Niyama, Mukti, and Seal as they moved along.

After some time, they came upon a long white house with bright blue shutters and doors.

"Let's try to get help there," Niyama said.

Mukti nodded, and they hurried forward. They couldn't tell if anyone was inside. Niyama shifted Seal's weight on his shoulder, then used his free paw to knock loudly. He and Mukti put their ears forward and listened intently.

Silence.

Niyama knocked again, more forcefully.

A creaking sound came from within.

Mukti leaned forward with hopeful eyes. Then came the sound of a metal bolt sliding, and the narrow wooden doors parted.

It was a langur! Six tiny fur-rimmed faces were pressed against each side of the tall langur who had opened the door. "Who is it, Papa?" the six children asked in unison.

"We need help," Niyama explained. "Our friend is hurt...and another is—" He couldn't finish his sentence for the tears choking his voice.

Concern crossed the langur's face, and he quickly stepped aside. "Come in, come in." He waved them forward. "Put your friend there." He pointed toward a small wooden bed in the corner, then he opened the window shutters above the bed.

Niyama gently laid Seal down.

The tall langur bent over her while the tiny langurs

crowded in to watch. They looked with great curiosity at Seal. They had never seen a white-and-gray cat
before. "Move back, little ones," the tall langur gently
directed. The six faces moved back, like a wave leaving
the shore.

Seal looked at them with a gentle joy. *So this is how
the langurs live.* She could see kindness and care in their
little faces. Her gaze went past them, and she noticed
that even though her eyes were open, she was feeling
the way she had in deep meditation. Very still and
quiet. The room seemed to be expanding before her.
Her body was undergoing some sort of change. The
pain had lessened, but she also noticed she couldn't
feel most of her body anymore. She was very weak,
and each breath was difficult.

The tall langur began gently and skillfully examining her.

Niyama and Mukti could tell he knew what he was
doing. "You're a doctor?" Mukti asked hopefully.

"Not by the law," the langur answered. "Here in
the mountain village, our ancestors taught us how to
care for ourselves. Other help would be too far away,"
he replied in soft tones.

"Our friend was attacked," Niyama explained.

"By Kadir," Mukti added. "She was trying to help
her friend escape."

They continued watching the mountain doctor with
worry and hope.

"Kadir!" the langur exclaimed, looking down into
Seal's eyes. "He's been causing trouble here for weeks.
Where is the friend?" The langur continued his work.

"Here," Niyama sadly replied as he took the small

cloth bundle containing Ardaas from his pack. "We need to take care of him properly," he said with a sob.

The langur gazed at the tiny cloth bundle and sighed in sadness, shaking his head. "We'll get things ready."

The tall langur finally stopped examining Seal and turned with a sorrowful gaze to Niyama and Mukti. "Her spine is broken," he said softly. "There's not much we can do but make her comfortable and wait…"

Mukti's and Niyama's faces were soaked with tears. They sat on the floor, huddled together.

The langur offered Seal some water. Feebly she sipped a few times, then fell into a deep slumber.

For some hours, Seal lay in stillness with her breath coming less and less. By the time evening had deepened the color of the sky, one last breath came from her muzzle. Then she lay still and silent.

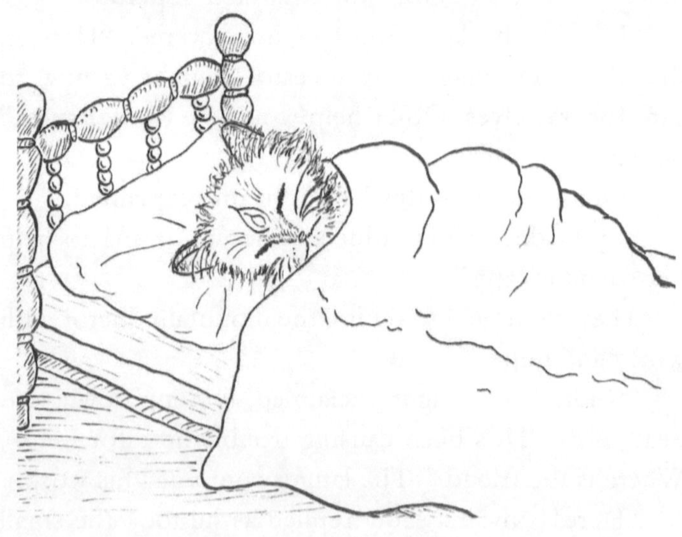

The next thing she knew, she seemed to be floating and looking down at her body as it lay lifeless in the bed. She could hear the conversation going on in the room.

"She has passed," the langur said in soft tones.

"It was her ninth incarnation," Mukti added as his head dropped down.

CHAPTER 27

LIFE AFTER DEATH

THE ROOM DISAPPEARED, AND A BLUESISH–WHITE brightness filled Seal's vision.

Then she experienced something like a movie playing in her mind. She watched as her whole life whizzed by, from kittenhood until the last few seconds in the

langur's cottage. Tansen's voice echoed in her mind, *"Time is running out, Seal!"*

Then all the images faded away. She was alone, very alone, but not lonely. Now, there was only an infinite, deep darkness, which felt like it was expanding. Her awareness sank down into the inky depths of nothingness. It was like a force of gravity was pulling her into this place that wasn't a place. It had no up or down, no front or back, no here or there. Yet Seal sensed that, somehow, this "nothing" contained the seed of everything.

After some time, the darkness was pierced by pinpoints of pure white light. The vastness of space and time seemed to be folding and unfolding within her awareness. She felt a deep, quiet stillness, and she knew what she felt was her true self. When death had taken her, something had remained. Fear was gone, pain was gone, her body was gone. She wasn't a she anymore. She wasn't a cat anymore. But she still was.

Where's Ardaas? she thought. *Did I fail again?* Then she began to feel Ardaas's presence, strongly. *Is he coming? Is he here?*

The brilliant pinpoints began to pulse with musical vibration. They were coming from all directions. She realized that Ardaas was in all of them. Not only that—so was she. It was all one. *Divine force in everything,* she thought. Good, bad, fear, love, gratitude, loss, life, and death. It was all in the light, and it was unspeakably beautiful. It was all perfect. All parts to one wholeness. Everything was there as the One.

Then Seal felt a choice arise. It didn't come as

words or thoughts, just as a feeling. She could sense an option of moving forward through the cold, white lights and on to stillness. It felt like it would be "going home" in the most final, complete way.

The other option she felt was like a pulling downward into the warmth and vibrations of life.

Which to choose?

Then Kadir suddenly came into her memory. She had seen the look of sadness and grief on his face before he had run from the cottage. *More than anything, I want for him to somehow feel the completeness and love that is filling me now,* she thought. *If Kadir could experience this wholeness, peace, and joy in his own heart, he wouldn't hurt anyone again. He wouldn't want to. His suffering would be over.* But was it possible?

Her cat body had been destroyed. It had been her ninth life. She knew it wasn't possible to reincarnate

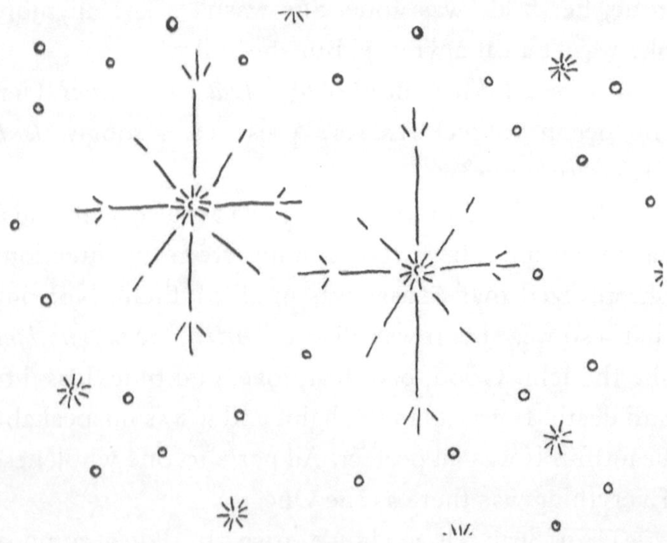

as her cat self any longer. But her powerful desire to share the experience of compassion, forgiveness, and love with Kadir had made the decision for her.

A shock of warmth ran through her awareness, and she felt her consciousness being sucked downward. It was like she was on a magic space slide. But what kind of body her soul might possibly end up in was a mystery.

CHAPTER 28

THE SACRIFICE

SUNSHINE RADIATED DOWN ON AN ANCIENT LEAFY TREE. Sheltered in it was a tiny, round nest. The sides were covered with a thin layer of soft green moss. Wind stirred the branches, moving them up and down. The little nest remained firmly attached to the thin branch it had been lovingly and painstakingly built upon.

A cracking sound came from within the nest. Long, thin beaks began to protrude from the eggs within. After some hours of pecking, two tiny birds lay exhausted in a pile of shell. When they saw each other, they smiled silently. Seal and Ardaas were together again.

Within a week, they sprouted their first pin feathers, which left them looking like porcupines. The two friends laughed at their funny appearance, then snuggled together as they quietly rested and grew.

"I'm so happy we're together again," she whispered to her companion.

"We're hummingbirds, Seal!" he told her with glee. "Soon, our wings will be strong enough to fly."

Seal wondered in amazement, *What in the world will soaring in the sky feel like?*

Their mother buzzed to and from the nest many times throughout the day. "This time, I have a momma taking care of me!" Seal whispered to her companion with joy. Their diligent caregiver worked hard to keep her little hatchlings fed. Every time she would appear, Ardaas and Seal would tip their beaks up toward the sky, making tiny chirping noises as she fed them.

The two friends remembered what had happened in their last lifetime. One afternoon, as they snuggled safely in their nest, they began talking about it.

"I had a vision. I saw that Kadir went through some horrible things when he was small," Seal explained to him. She told him all she had seen, and how he, Ardaas, had died in that lifetime along with the gorilla's whole family.

"Kadir was my little ape friend?" Ardaas exclaimed in shock. "I didn't know." He became quiet as he considered this new revelation. "The cruel monster he grew into is nothing like the loving companion I used to swing through the trees with…" His voice trailed off as he cried. He silently thought some moments longer, then said, "I think what those humans did made Kadir go crazy. He had so much sadness and anger in his heart that he couldn't heal from it."

"Yeah," Seal replied with sorrow, "it was too much pain. He wasn't able to heal."

After that, the two friends began to meditate.

Forty days after they had hatched, the little nest buzzed with great activity. Seal and Ardaas now had proper hummingbird feathers.

"It feels like I am in a beautiful costume!" Seal exclaimed as she held her wings out, turning this way and that in the sunshine. Her throat was ruby red, and her wings shone with shimmering green feathers.

Gracefully, they buzzed up into the sky, savoring the experience of this new life. Seal marveled at how wonderful it felt to have wings and fly through the air at lightning speed. They giggled as they practiced whizzing and stopping in midair or changing directions on a dime. The friends flew through sun and shade, leafy trees and rolling fields of wildflowers. They paused at a vine with purple nectar-filled blossoms and filled their tummies with the sweet, nutritious liquid.

One evening, as they settled back into their nest after a long day of exploring, they talked of Kadir again.

"Ardaas, what if there's something we can do for him?"

"I'd give anything to help him. He was once my best friend."

The next day, Seal and Ardaas didn't go exploring. Instead, they stayed in their nest and meditated in silent stillness for a long while. During that quiet time, their souls went on a shared journey.

"Look, Seal! There's Kadir. He's in the jungle."

"Watch for landmarks," she instructed. "That's how we'll know how to find him."

"He's still in the Himalayas," Ardaas said. "He's in a forest, below a cave. It seems like a sacred place. I keep hearing the sounds of bells."

"There's a temple gate near the road with a huge brass bell hanging from it," Seal observed. "But what does the sign say? It's in another language."

"That's Hindi," Ardaas replied. "I must remember it from one of my past lives." He smiled. "It says, 'Way to Kasar Devi Mandir.' That means the temple," he explained. Then he asked Seal, "What will we do to help him?"

"Somehow, we have to share this energy of love with him," she reasoned.

They sat together, considering what to do. Then, the two friends became silent and went deeper into their meditation. When they opened their eyes, they smiled at each other. They had formulated a plan. But it would cost them their lives.

The next morning, they went out to feed on orange blossoms. This would be their fuel for the long journey ahead. Then they took rest, snuggling together in the nest one last time.

When they awoke, Seal chirped, "Ready, Ardaas?"

"Absolutely, Seal!"

प्रवेशद्वार
कसारदेवी
मंदिर

They flew a great distance. Through trees, streets, villages, farmland, and, finally, the thickest jungle. The two birds weaved and soared, waves of color through the sky. After some time, they began following a narrow, curving mountain road.

"I hear the bell!" Seal cried out happily.

Ardaas smiled as they rounded a bend.

There, next to the road, stood the red temple gate labeled Kasar Devi. Gliding under the arch, the tiny birds continued up the forested pathway.

Soon, they came to a hovering pause under the low-branching trees. A large, dark, furry mass was slumped over in the damp shadows. It was Kadir. His head was hanging downward. He wore a hauntingly vacant stare that spoke of sorrow, loneliness, and desolation.

Fluttering their wings steadily, the two friends surveyed the scene.

"There he is, Ardaas. Do you think we can do it?"

"I don't know. But let's give it a try."

The little hummingbirds began a moving meditation. Their tiny wings beat faster and faster as they let their minds relax into deep stillness. The audible buzz they produced was now creating a strange humming music in the air. A change was beginning in their little bodies, which were now shining with pure white light. They continued to focus as they hovered above Kadir.

Soon they became so bright that it made Kadir look up. He shaded his eyes, gazing up at the two tiny spots above him. They were as bright as the sun. He seemed puzzled by the sight before him.

Seal and Ardaas looked at each other one final time

before their hummingbird bodies dissolved into pure energy and love. The buzzing sound of their wings stopped, and their brightness intensified even more. The two orbs shot directly toward Kadir like rockets, straight into his chest in a shower of sparks—vibration of the *naad*, a pulse of energy from the Divine. They had entered into Kadir's heart center as pure love.

Kadir felt like the wind had been knocked out of him. He looked down at his chest to see if he'd been hurt, but the little suns had left no visible mark. A physical warmth was growing in his chest. It grew and grew until it seemed like his whole being was radiating, ready to burst.

His heart was pounding. *What are these feelings that are coming with the warmth?* he wondered, afraid.

Tears were streaming down his face, and sobs shook his body uncontrollably. Intuitively, he knew to let it all out. *It feels like I am being cleaned on the inside,* he thought in amazement. All the horror of his childhood as well as the countless cruel things he had done to others came before him. Everything was acknowledged, then let go of.

For hours, Kadir continued sitting in silent stillness under the trees. Waves of deep peace, love, contentment…even happiness had begun moving through his entire being. But most surprising of all, he became aware of feeling forgiven for all the painful things he had done—so many mistakes and wrong turns, and all the suffering he had caused in his blind rage. He felt it all being washed away, as if some cosmic doctor was slowly bathing his heart and mind in love until it became completely clean and pure.

How could these beautiful things be in me? he wondered.

Gentle tears trickled down his dirt-stained face, which for the first time in many lifetimes wore a faint smile.

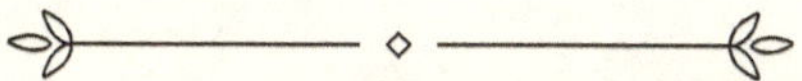

Many years of sorrow, inner pain, and violence had ravaged Kadir's body with disease and weakness. He continued silently resting in the sacred jungle, watching the small forest creatures with wonder and innocence.

A few days after receiving the gift from the two tiny suns, his soul departed peacefully one morning before dawn.

EPILOGUE

Mukti, Niyama, and Tansen were walking together around the marble *parkarma* of the *Sarovar*. Tansen had returned to India quickly once he heard what had happened.

The Golden Temple was illumined by the deepening sunset. The waves of the sacred pool vibrated with gleaming ripples. Music floated from the temple windows, surrounding the friends with the holy sound current.

"Tansen, did Seal run out of time? Was it too late?" Mukti asked with concern.

"I would say her timing was perfection," he answered with a soft smile as a tear rolled down his cheek.

They continued walking along.

Tansen paused, pointing to a trio of playful hummingbirds buzzing near the edge of the shimmering water, in the shade of one of the sacred trees. "Look"—he chuckled—"three friends…"

Mukti and Niyama looked up and smiled at the sight of the beautiful tiny birds playing together.

They continued in silence for some time until they reached a patch of tulsi. Mukti paused, pushing his nose down to smell the fragrant leaves, his beard draping on the ground.

"Mukti?" Tansen asked in an inquisitive tone.

"Yes, sir?" Mukti answered, looking up.

"Excuse me for asking, but is that beard fake?"

THE END

Yes, there was a real Seal.
Her life was adventurous and deep.
She was greatly loved, and her presence is missed.

ACKNOWLEDGMENTS

THANK YOU TO ALL THOSE WHO BELIEVED IN ME AND encouraged me to finish this work.

Special thanks to Raj Giandeep Singh (Tosh N. Hatch), for your generous support in the creation of this book and for your willingness to read and re-read my early drafts. Thank you also for your helpful input on the illustrations. Your honest feedback was invaluable. This book would not have been possible without you. I am ever grateful for your friendship and presence in my life.

Gratitude and blessings to my teacher, Dr. Narinder Singh Sandhu (Ustad Ji), for inspiring my music, my life, and for believing in this project. Thank you for all the ways in which you have taught me and for your never-failing faith in me. Your high standards for my progress have enabled me to come into my own deep relationship with music, as well as an ever-growing, rich proficiency in the Punjabi language.

Big thanks to Harpreet Singh and Samia Sandhu

for guiding me to Grambells in Chandigarh and letting me stay with you while I completed my work there.

Thank you to Bir Taj Singh, Brahm Mauli Kaur, Xavier and Kendall Luker, Mehtab Kaur, and Wahenoor Singh for being my playmates and reminding me why I love writing for children in the first place.

Thank you to my art teacher and friend, Sophia Esterman, for your inspiration and guidance. Thank you for helping me brainstorm about mediums for the illustrations and for gifting me the pens, nibs, and ink that gave birth to the artwork in this book.

Thank you to Debra L. Hartmann and her team at The Pro Book Editor for helping me bring the best version of this work to the world.

Thank you to the numerous spiritual teachers and traditions that have informed and transformed my life. Most of all, thank you to the Great Divine - Waheguru, from whom this story truly flows.

ABOUT THE AUTHOR

Amanjot Kaur grew up in Salt Lake City, Utah, surrounded by the Rocky Mountains and the Great Salt Lake. Meditation and yoga have been part of her life for over 20 years. Her time living in India while studying Indian Classical music as well as visits to Japan and Nepal cultivated a deep love of foreign cultures, which she delights in bringing to life through her art and writing. Her first novel, *The Ninth Incarnation*, incorporates elements of Eastern spiritual practice with an adventure story for young adults and all those young at heart.

Besides her writing, painting, and illustrating, Amanjot is a musician, certified yoga instructor, Reiki practitioner, and an accomplished seamstress. She continues traveling to India where she studies Hindustani Classical music and Gurmat Sangeet with Dr. Narinder Singh Sandhu.

Currently residing in rural Connecticut, Amanjot spends her free time hiking in the forests of New England, studying Punjabi, and hanging out with her landlady's cat, Shadow.

To join our mailing list, please visit:
www.AmanjotAbroad.com